SARAH LEAN grew up in Wells, Somerset but now lives in Dorset with her husband, son and dog. She has worked as a page-planner for a newspaper, a stencil-maker and a gardener, amongst various other things. She gained a first-class English degree and became a primary school teacher before returning to complete an MA in Creative and Critical Writing with University of Winchester. *The Forever Whale* is Sarah's third novel for children.

Also by Sarah Lean

A Dog Called Homeless

Winner of the Hazelgrove Book Award and the
prestigious Schneider Family Middle School Book Award
in the US. Shortlisted for the Sheffield Children's Book
Award and longlisted for the Branford Boase Award.

"Heartbreakingly beautiful... I loved it."
Cathy Cassidy

"An exceptional debut... richly characterized."
The Sunday Times

"Genuinely moving and beautifully written."
The Bookseller

A Horse for Angel

SARAH LEAN

The
Forever
Whale

Illustrated by Gary Blythe

HarperCollins *Children's Books*

First published in Great Britain by HarperCollins *Children's Books* in 2013
HarperCollins *Children's Books* is a division of HarperCollins*Publishers* Ltd,
77-85 Fulham Palace Road, Hammersmith, London, W6 8JB.

The HarperCollins website address is: www.harpercollins.co.uk

1

Copyright © Sarah Lean 2013
Illustrations © Gary Blythe 2013

ISBN 978-0-00-751222-5

Sarah Lean asserts the moral right to be identified
as the author of the work.
Gary Blythe asserts the moral right to be identified
as the illustrator of the work.

Printed and bound in England by Clays Ltd, St Ives plc.

MIX
Paper from
responsible sources
FSC www.fsc.org **FSC™ C007454**

FSC™ is a non-profit international organisation established to promote
the responsible management of the world's forests. Products carrying the
FSC label are independently certified to assure consumers that they come
from forests that are managed to meet the social, economic and
ecological needs of present and future generations,
and other controlled sources.

Find out more about HarperCollins and the environment at
www.harpercollins.co.uk/green

For Edward, who filmed our home and showed me his point of view... and the cat's

1.

GRANDAD DRAWS THE OARS INTO THE BOAT as we coast on the glassy water until we nudge into the bank. We both have our fingers over our lips, not to tell each other to be quiet, because we are, but because we think alike. I don't know what Grandad has seen, I only know to trust him.

"Can you see it, Hannah?" Grandad whispers.

The dappled and striped shadows are barely moving in the golden September evening and I can't see anything in the jumble of grasses and reeds. I shake my head.

"Keep looking," Grandad whispers.

I follow his eyes, but it takes me a long while to spot the fawn, curled up and waiting. Its skin is hardly any different from the landscape around it. I can see the glisten of its black nose, but it knows to stay still, to be safe. Once I see it, it stands out a mile.

I whisper, "Is the fawn all right on its own, Grandad?"

He nods his head towards another curve of the bank. A deer is looking at us, anxious because she doesn't want to draw attention to her fawn, who is separated from her by a channel of water.

Grandad smiles to himself. "Will you stay or

will you swim across?" He says it as if he and the deer have a history together. We've seen deer here many times, but he's never said that before.

"I didn't know deer could swim," I say, keeping my voice low and soft like his.

"That's how they came to live on…" Grandad hesitates and looks over his shoulder. His eyebrows are crushed into a frown. He's looking towards the island in the middle of the huge harbour, even though we can barely see it from here. But I'm not sure why.

"Furze Island?" I ask.

"Furze Island," he repeats. "A long time ago a herd of deer swam over from the mainland and settled on the island."

Grandad is still looking far away towards the harbour entrance, maybe for the billow of sails, to see if any broad and magnificent ships have blown in today.

We are quiet for a few minutes until Grandad speaks again. "It's your turn to row now," he says.

We change places in the boat. I see him stumble. He must be tired today. Grandad and I have taken a thousand journeys like this out in the quiet inlets of the harbour. Here we are just specks, tiny people marvelling at the changing sea and all the ordinary everyday things. These are my favourite days. I feel the familiar tug in my middle as the oars knock in their sockets and I row, pulling, rolling and lifting like Grandad taught me. The paddles splash like a slow-ticking clock.

"Hannah, I want you to remember something for me," Grandad says. "Something important, in case I forget."

I wonder why he would ever forget something

important, but I want him to tell me.

"Anything for you," I say.

"August the eighteenth," he says. "You'll remind me, won't you?"

"That's a long time away, nearly a year. Are you going somewhere?"

I only ask because I know that Grandad has spent all his life here in Hambourne, working with wood, rowing the inlets with me, and watching from his bedroom window for schooners and square-riggers in the harbour.

Grandad leans against the side of the boat and scratches his white beard and the bristles crackle under his fingernails. His eyes are warm and brown like oiled wood.

"Some journeys need us to travel great distances. But others are closer to home, like today when our eyes see more than what's in front of us."

"You mean like finding the fawn in the grass?"
I see his face folding like worn origami paper into
the peaceful shape I've always known.

Grandad slowly puts his gnarly old hand on the
bench between us. My hand is still smooth like a
map without journeys and I put it on top of his.
We pile our hands over each other, his then mine,

his then mine, like we always have. He pulls his huge hands out and gathers mine like an apple in his. And, just like always, that feeling is too big to keep inside me and bursts out and makes me laugh.

"Yes, great journeys like this," he says. "Those great days that live in our memories and make us who we are."

I'm not sure I exactly understand what he means. I just see something in him and I want to be like him too. Somewhere there in his sun-baked skin is a map of everything that made him who he is.

"Can I come with you on August the eighteenth, Grandad? I want to see what you've seen."

Grandad's ancient smile fills his cheeks and his eyes and I think of his face as a whole life-full of memories.

"It's all right here." His huge hand is over his chest. "The greatest power on earth. Remember, you have to think big, Hannah, and when things are good, think bigger."

Grandad moved in with us after Grandma died ten years ago. I wasn't exactly here then, still wriggling and growing into a baby inside my mum, but our home was his before it was mine.

Grandad hadn't liked to live alone and Mum hadn't wanted him to live alone either. Grandma, who I never met, had done everything for him. She'd pressed his shirts and cooked his tea and put a cushion behind his head when he fell asleep in the chair. Even though he could have done all of these things for himself, she'd thought of him before she did anything.

I'm named after her. She was Hannah Jenkins, I'm Hannah Gray, and in lots of ways I'm like her.

Just then a voice calls across the water. Dad is waiting for us on the slope at Gorbreen slipway. It's late, he's saying; he's telling us to come ashore.

I pull on one oar to steer us in.

Dad steadies Grandad as he climbs out and tells Grandad he should sit in the car, but he stays by the slipway and stares out to the harbour again. Dad and I roll the trailer under the boat. We pull it up the slipway and I leave Dad to hitch it to the car.

I stand beside Grandad and wonder why he's not getting in the car.

"I think it's time to put the boat away for the winter, Hannah," he says.

I know this means we won't go out rowing again until next spring.

A curlew is singing, and it's soft and eerie, filling the bay and my ears.

"Grandad, tell me more about the deer," I say.

Grandad nods and smiles, but he's looking at the footprints of seabirds pressed in the soft muddy bank. They'll be washed away when the tide comes in and draws out again.

"Come on, you two," Dad calls. "Time to go."

There's a long moment before we go, when I see into Grandad's warm eyes and he says, "I have

quite a story I'm saving to tell you about the deer."
He says it quietly so only I hear his deep voice
through the curlew's song.

"Remember August the eighteenth," he says
again. "And one day, I hope you'll go on the
journey and see what I saw."

2.

"READY FOR SOME TOAST, GRANDAD?"

Grandad likes his toast cooked under the gas grill so it's dark brown with charcoal around the edge.

"I've got it," I say because Grandad is staring blankly at the kitchen cupboards. I've already found the bread knife and cut an extra piece of bread as always.

"Watch the toast a minute," I say and go outside to feed the birds.

Every morning I still try to do what Grandad and I have always done because it's helping his memory stay alive. We haven't been out in the boat again for nearly a year, but there are lots of other everyday things that we've always shared. Our early mornings are special, even though things are not exactly the same as they used to be.

Grandad has Alzheimer's disease. One moment he is as he's always been, wise and knowing and safe. Sometimes his memory fades like a ship disappearing into a sea mist.

Alzheimer's usually picks on older people, but it's not fussy about things like how big or bold a person is, or how important they are to their granddaughter. It's taking all the things Grandad learned, all the things he saw and heard, all the things he loved. Alzheimer's is a history thief, stealing his past and our future together.

The hedges shiver with excited twittering as I sprinkle the crusts on the lawn and as soon as I step back the sparrows get busy with the crumbs. I turn the earth with the garden fork that Grandad always leaves there. The robin comes and perches on the fork handle and watches the soil for the wriggle of a worm or centipede. Grandad once said

that an ounce of brown and red feathers didn't seem like much, but it's the robin's nature to be fierce like a tiger when it protects its territory. He likes the robin most of all.

I water our sunflowers. They're taller than me, but the heads are still fresh and green. I can remember Grandad and I crouched in our wellies the first time we grew them. He'd shown me some small black and white striped seeds, shaped like miniature rowing boats.

"See this tiny little package?" he'd said, drawing away one of the seeds with his fingertip. "All it needs is water and the sun and in a few short months it will become a giant. And, when it's a giant, it will have its own tiny seeds and each one can become a giant too."

"Like it goes on forever?" I'd said.

"Just like that, only in a new plant."

We'd pressed our seeds into pots of compost and I waited for them to grow. I hadn't known what to expect and asked him every day when I came back from school where the giants were. Until I saw them for myself.

But even when the leaves turned dark and the stalks were thick with sap and towered over me, I still had to wait for the new seeds to ripen so that we could store them and then, the following spring, press them into the compost to grow once again.

Grandad follows me outside. I notice he doesn't have his slippers on, but it doesn't matter because the June summer ground is dry and warm.

I've asked Grandad the same question every day for years, even though I know the answer. I ask him again now: "When will the sunflower seeds be ready?" But this is the first morning he doesn't reply. I say it for him: "When the hearts are golden," so that one of us remembers.

Grandad nods towards the hard shadow of the fence in the far corner of our garden where a cat is twitching its tail. He struggles to remember the cat's name.

"It's Smokey," I say, even though I'm sure Grandad will remember in a minute.

"Yes, that's it," he says. "We can try and keep the birds safe from him, but Smokey can't help being a dog."

I know Grandad meant to say cat not dog. Sometimes the Alzheimer's makes him muddle things up, but I usually know what he means.

Smokey is a clever grey cat, and I've seen him catch baby sparrows before. Even though Mrs Simm gives him plenty of food, Smokey will take a bird if he wants to. I think of Smokey like he's

Alzheimer's disease, creeping in and stealing things that don't belong to him.

I hiss and Smokey scrabbles over the fence.

Grandad opens the garage door and he's trying to untie the tarpaulin over his boat.

"Fair and fine today," he smiles. "Shall we launch at Gorbreen?"

I don't remind him we haven't been in the boat since we put it away at the end of last September. I don't tell him Dad won't let us go out any more. "I'll sort the boat out, Grandad. We could go and see the deer again." And I lead him away, back into the garden.

"Grandad? Remember you were going to tell me a story?" I say. He doesn't reply. An ocean of nothing washes into his eyes. "A story about the deer? About a journey?"

This isn't the first time I've asked him. It isn't

the first time I've reminded him of the months passing. August 18th is now only eight weeks away.

"Journey?" he says. "Where are we going?"

Suddenly the smoke alarm shrills from the kitchen.

"Grandad, the toast!"

I run back inside. Smoke curls out of the grill and rolls up to the ceiling. I turn off the gas, climb on to the kitchen table and jump up to try to turn the alarm off before anyone else comes down for breakfast, but I'm not tall enough to reach.

Mum runs down the stairs. She stands on a chair and pokes at the alarm with a broom handle until it stops shrieking.

"Watch what Grandad's doing, please," Mum whispers as we try to wave the smoke away with tea towels.

"It was just an accident," I say when Dad comes in.

Dad looks out at Grandad in the garden and I know what he's thinking.

"It's my fault," I say. "I was feeding the birds and chasing Smokey away and watering the sunflowers and I forgot about the breakfast."

"Sounds like you've had a busy morning," Dad says.

He opens the fridge to get some juice and finds his car keys in there. He takes them out and bounces them up and down in his hand.

"Will you put those boxes by the front door into the car?" Mum says to Dad. "I'll be along in a minute." He and Mum share a long look before Mum says to him, "We'll talk later."

"Save some energy for school, Hannah," Dad says on his way out.

Grandad comes into the kitchen. He opens the cupboard under the sink and pulls out a bag of birdseed. He doesn't say anything about the smoke and the toast, he doesn't close the cupboard door and the bag of seed is tipping from his hands.

"Grandad," Mum says, "they're spilling and going everywhere!" Dots of seed bounce up from the tiled floor around his feet. "Grandad?"

Grandad doesn't seem to hear her and shuffles back outside, leaving a trail of seeds behind him. I hear the sparrows twittering, waiting for him.

"How is he this morning?" Mum says, sniffing at the bitter smell of burnt toast on her sleeve.

"He's fine," I say. "I heard him get up in the night so he's probably just tired." Mum frowns. "I can sweep that up," I say, jumping down and reaching for the broom.

Mum holds on to the handle for a moment.

"Hannah…" she says, but I don't want her to say what everybody in our house has been saying recently, that they're worried about the way Grandad is behaving.

"He's fine," I say again. "*I* forgot about the toast. It's *my* fault."

Mum sighs a little and says, "Go and help Grandad, love."

"Mum!" I point to the toast on fire in the cooker behind her.

Mum steps down from the chair and uses the barbecue tongs to pick up the flaming toast and fling it out of the back door, and while she isn't looking I close the door to the cupboard under the sink because I've noticed that there are things inside it that shouldn't be there.

3.

"WHAT WAS THAT ALL ABOUT?" MY SISTER JODIE says, when Mum has gone to work. "And what's that disgusting smell?"

I'm on the floor with a brush, but the seeds keep bouncing back out of the dustpan.

"I forgot to watch the toast," I mutter.

Jodie pretends she doesn't see me sweep some of the seeds under the doormat.

"Why don't you just use the toaster like everyone else?" she says, painting gloss on her lips.

I bite my teeth together. "Why can't Grandad have it how he likes it?"

Jodie doesn't say anything. She's more interested in smudging her lips and watching her reflection on the edge of the cooker.

"Why are you putting on lipgloss before you've had your breakfast?" I say.

She rolls her eyes and pours some cereal and milk and mutters to herself, "Where's he put the sugar bowl now?"

Jodie sighs and goes out of the kitchen because the last time the bowl wasn't by the kettle we eventually found it in a drawer in the sitting room. These things are Alzheimer's fault, not Grandad's.

I crawl across the floor and open the cupboard under the sink. It smells of damp. The sugar bowl is there, but it has tipped over the bags and bags of birdseed stuffed inside. I think about putting the bowl over by the kettle, but Jodie has come back and is watching me.

"What's that in there?" she says.

I close the door, but Jodie comes over, so I push her away and sit with my back against the cupboard door with my arms folded and my legs crossed.

"Actually, this is my place for hiding private things," I tell her, "so leave them alone."

She stands with her legs either side of me and I make myself go all stiff, but it doesn't work because she's fifteen and five years bigger and stronger than me.

"Don't be a baby," Jodie says.

She holds my elbows, pulls me away and opens the door. She finds an old tube of sparkly lipstick,

Grandad's slippers and one of her books that went missing a few weeks ago. She leaves the cupboard door open and slides down to the floor, wiping sticky sugar crystals from her lipstick.

"*I* put those things in there when I was sweeping," I say.

She holds the book in front of my face. The damp pages bulge.

"Sure you did." Jodie twitches her mouth to the side. "I know what you're trying to do, but it's not like we don't all know Grandad's getting worse."

I grit my teeth again and then take a minute because I want Jodie on my side. "I notice things more than anyone else. He's tired today, that's all. Can't he just have a bad day like everyone else? He'll be fine later, you'll see."

Jodie twiddles with her hair and we sit in silence with my words still echoing in my own ears because I know they're not true. It's what I want to believe though.

Jodie reaches inside the cupboard and finds four bars of chocolate.

"Grandad's still hiding his chocolate, like a squirrel hides nuts for the winter," she says. She doesn't want to fight either. "Even before he got Alzheimer's he'd forget where he put it."

"Remember that time I ate so much of Grandad's chocolate that I was sick?" I say.

We laugh quietly together.

I remember that night when Jodie and I had snuck around the house with a torch to look for Grandad's hidden chocolate. We'd found loads and then hidden under the kitchen table. I ate far too much. Jodie knocked on Grandad's bedroom door because we knew Mum and Dad would make a fuss, but Grandad would just put things right.

He'd sent Jodie to bed and sat me on his lap in his high-backed chair with a bowl and a towel until I felt better.

"Did you know your grandma liked chocolate when she was a little girl?" he'd asked me as he wrapped us both in a blanket and took the bowl away from under my chin.

I shook my head through my tears. He smiled and his eyes crinkled.

"She had a sweet tooth like you, that's why I've always had to hide my chocolate."

"Did you marry her when she was a little girl?" I sniffed.

He chuckled quietly. "No, but even then I knew she was the girl for me."

"How did you know?" I'd asked. He rubbed my back and I felt the sickness going and sleep on its way.

"How did I know? Well, that's simple. Because something great put us together, bound us together forever, and it will never be undone."

I remember tucking my head into his shoulder.

"What was the great thing?"

I remember feeling his wide chest heave as he took in a giant breath. I remember the dark and the quiet and the glimmer of light from the hall. I remember him saying, "Another time. Go to sleep now, little Hannah."

4.

Jodie nudges me. "Hello? Where were you?"

I was thinking about the story Grandad had been meaning to tell me, wondering if it had anything to do with Grandma. I want him to remember because August 18th is getting closer, but no matter how many times I've said it, he doesn't know why he asked me to remind him. None of us have birthdays on that day, no anniversaries, nothing like that, I checked. I think it must be to do with a memory Grandad has, something important that scoops him up and takes him back to another time so he can feel those things that happened all over again.

I think of how important it is for all of us, but especially for Grandad, to remember the bright things from the past. There must have been so many of them to make him so special, or maybe just one extraordinary thing. I hate that Alzheimer's doesn't always let him go back to times and places he loved the most, when I can, just like that, if I want to.

I'm still on the kitchen floor with Jodie.

"Do you remember Grandma?" I ask her.

"Not much." Jodie looks disappointed with herself for a moment. "She had soft cheeks, that's what I remember, and she always had toffees in her cardigan pocket. You could hear the papers rustling." She pinches my cheek and pushes a chocolate bar into my hands. "You're little and soft like Grandma was," she smiles.

Grandad comes into the kitchen. "Time for breakfast," he says.

"I'll make you some more toast, Grandad," I say.

I cut some more bread, put it in the toaster this time and turn the timer up high.

"My class is going on a field trip down to the quay today," I tell him as we sit to eat our toast. "The mayor is unveiling a statue of a lifeboat. They've put a big cover over it so nobody can see it until today. Would you like to go down at the weekend and see it too?"

Slowly Grandad turns towards me. "We'll hide

my boat at Hambourne where nobody will find it."

Right then I feel as if I'm on my own in the boat at sea, and I can't see solid land on the horizon, and there's nowhere safe to go. I'm about to tell Grandad that his boat is in the garage, but sometimes when I correct what he says he gets confused and I don't want to upset him.

The dark edges of his toast crumble and fall into his lap. He doesn't notice.

"Hannah," Jodie says, breaking the uncomfortable silence, "we'd better get going."

She picks up her bulging book and some photographs fall out from between the pages and scatter on the table. Three are of my grandma, Hannah Jenkins, who I never knew; three are of me, Hannah Gray. All of the photos are rippled and flaking from the dampness in the cupboard.

Grandad's eyebrows furrow as we all look at the photos.

"Where's Hannah?" he says. "I haven't seen her this morning."

Jodie stares at me, chewing the pad of her thumb. I try to hide what feels like a stone dropping in my stomach. She doesn't say what I know she's thinking, that neither of us knows whether he's forgotten that Grandma died over ten years ago or if he's now starting to forget me.

Jodie goes to the front door, but I can't leave, not yet. I want to believe that when I come back this afternoon Grandad will be as he always was. I lean my hand on the table and kiss the white beard on his cheek.

"We're going to school now," I say.

His eyes brighten for a moment and he doesn't

know what he's just said, but I see something unfamiliar in his face.

"Grandad, please remember the story you were going to tell me. About the deer, about a journey. It'll be August the eighteenth soon."

His eyes flicker as if he's searching for something. He rubs his beard and I hear the bristles. I see brightness in his eyes, as if he's found something.

"Hannah!" Jodie calls. "We're going to be late!"

Grandad moves his hand and mine disappears underneath his.

"It's quite a story, Hannah, about the greatest power on earth."

I'm not sure if we can wait until August.

"Hannah, you have to come now!" Jodie shouts.

"Tell me about it after school, Grandad," I say and kiss him again. "Today!"

"Today, after school, I'll be waiting," he says. "Let's see if we can find that whale."

"A whale?" I say, but Jodie has come back in and is dragging me away. "A whale, Grandad?" I call.

"Don't forget," I hear him say.

5.

THE MAYOR'S GOLD CHAIN LOOKS HEAVY, AND AT last he stops talking to the crowd and holds up a huge pair of scissors to cut the red ribbon around the statue. Four people are behind him, holding the corners of a big shiny black sheet so nobody can see what's underneath.

Josh Beale makes a noise like he's dying for some unknown reason, so our teacher tells him to shush, but he carries on gargling. I want to blank him out because I'm trying to think about what Grandad said this morning. I thought he wanted to tell me an important story about the deer, but he said we were going to find a whale. I don't understand. I'm thinking about how Alzheimer's disease is making me confused too.

A photographer from the local paper tells the mayor to wait a minute.

"Can we have some kids from the local school up there as well?" he says. "And a teacher."

I am one of the children who get picked and we line up either side of the mayor and pretend we're helping to hold the ribbon.

Everyone counts down, three, two, one. The scissors snip.

The four people let go of the cover and it billows above our heads, puffed up by the sea breeze. I feel the cool shadow over me as it ripples over our heads, falls and shrouds us. For a second the world goes dark and I smell something metallic. The people who were holding on to the cover drag it away again and everything seems just as it was. The crowd gasp then clap, but I have a funny feeling, like someone is standing behind me.

I turn round. The life-size statue is of a smooth golden-bronze figure, with no nose or eyes or mouth. It is leaning over the bow of a boat and reaching an arm to someone who is in the sea who doesn't have a proper face either.

"Hey, you, little girl," the photographer says, "look this way. Everyone smile."

I can't stop looking at the statue of the people with no faces. I see how hard the person in the boat is reaching for the one lost at sea.

I nudge Linus Drew who is standing next to me.

"Who is it?" I ask him.

"Who's who?" he says.

"The statues. How are we supposed to know who they are if they don't have faces?"

Linus shrugs, which is what he does a lot of the time. Our teacher hears me.

"They represent anyone," Mrs Gooch says. "We'll be talking about it later in class and reflecting on what we feel about the statue."

I think of Grandad and how this morning he looked at me but didn't see me. It feels like the shadow of the black cover is still over me.

"Anyone?" I say, catching Mrs Gooch's arm. "How can a person be anyone? Surely they have to be someone?"

"Well, yes, that's a good question, but this is art, Hannah, so there might be lots of possible meanings. Maybe we can find something of ourselves in it." Mrs Gooch waits for me to say something. "Is everything all right?" she asks.

I nod. But it's not true. Everything isn't all right and I want to talk about it, but I've not told anyone that my grandad has Alzheimer's. All my friends know him because of all the years he used to take me to and from school. He was the BFG at the school gates who lifted us up high in his arms and asked us to tell him what we'd been doing that day. I had told my friends Grandad didn't come any more because we'd got too big and because I could walk to school on my own now.

Alzheimer's isn't like a broken leg or the flu; it's buried in someone's brain. You can't see it. You just notice what's missing. People don't like it when it's something to do with brains and not being normal.

We line up to go back to school and I'm

partnered with my friend Megan. Mrs Gooch walks beside us.

"Megan?" Mrs Gooch says. "What did you think of the statue?"

"I thought it was nice because it's to remember all the people who helped save lives at sea," Megan says.

"Yes, it is. And how does it make you feel?"

I'm listening, but I don't really want to join in now.

"I feel… like it's good that we have people who will help us if we need them. And," Megan continues, "it reminds me that I have to wear a life jacket when we go out in my uncle's boat."

"So it also reminds you of something to do with yourself. What about you, Hannah?" Mrs Gooch says. I look back at the statue, at the people who could be anyone.

"I don't like that they don't have names," I say. "I want to know who they are."

Is it just my name that Grandad is forgetting? Or is it much more than that? What about all our journeys in his boat, all our thousands of mornings, our talks, all the things that tie us together? Will he remember the story? Will he remember me when I get home?

6.

"GRANDAD?" I CALL AFTER SCHOOL, WHILE I FLICK on the kettle for him. I'm still thinking about the statue on the quay. Mrs Gooch said we could all try and find something of ourselves in the statue, but I'm thinking of Grandad instead.

The back door is open. At first I think I see ashes outside on the patio, and I remember the burnt toast from this morning. But they aren't ashes. They're tiny red and brown feathers.

My stomach turns to stone. I call Grandad's name and run upstairs and look in all the rooms, but I'm already thinking that Smokey wouldn't dare come so close to the house to take a bird if Grandad was here.

I come back to the kitchen. Grandad's newspaper isn't on the table.

Grandad doesn't walk as well as he did, but most days he used to go as far as the shop down Southbrook Hill to get a bar of chocolate and a newspaper and some birdseed. On the way to the shop he'd stop to talk to Mr Howard who clips his box hedges with tiny shears into Christmas puddings and cones and clouds.

I run down the street. Mr Howard is clipping his hedge as usual.

"Have you seen my grandad today?" I call.

"Yes, he was headed thataway." Mr Howard points with his sharp snippers towards Southbrook Hill. "I wished him a good afternoon, but he walked past without so much as a friendly word. I told him he looked a little peaky, but… well, that was nearly an hour ago."

I am already running towards the hill.

Grandad isn't at the shop. Suddenly my mind is racing, thinking of how he was when I left this morning. Had he heard me after all? Would he have gone to see the statue at the quay by himself? I take the road that leads down to the old town.

Papers rustle and tumble along the cobbled street, blown by the sea breeze coming through an alleyway between the shops. At the end of the alleyway I stop to catch my breath and look both ways. I hear boat masts clanking along the quay like alarms. In the distance I see Grandad shuffling unsteadily away from the new statue towards Hambourne slipway. I keep running.

Coming towards Grandad from the opposite direction I see Megan, Josh and Linus, who is on his scooter. As they pass Grandad, they speak to him. Megan watches over her shoulder, but Grandad doesn't turn round so she stops and walks back to him. He looks down at the slipway, then out to sea.

"Grandad?" I call as I reach him. "What are you doing here?"

I hook my arm through his. He looks down at his other clenched hand. The ocean of nothing is in his eyes.

"Come on," I say. "You've walked all the way to Hambourne slipway. Let's go home now."

I try to lead him away, but his arm is heavy. Megan, Josh and Linus stand uncomfortably nearby. "What's wrong with him?" I hear Josh say to Linus.

"Grandad?" I say. "Let's walk home together."

"Do you want us to go?" Megan says.

But they don't go and I can't think what to do.

"Mr Jenkins," Linus says. "Hannah and me will walk you home."

Linus lays down his scooter and tries to take Grandad's other arm.

"This way," he says, but Grandad trembles.

"Grandad, please, it's me, Hannah," I say as a tear falls from his eye. "You're safe."

"Shall I get someone to help?" Megan says.

He's fine, I want to say. But I see the unstoppable grey-green tide rushing away from the slipway steps, in the same way that Alzheimer's is dragging Grandad away from me. Grandad doesn't know who I am.

"Grandad, it's me, Hannah. Remember, we're going to go on a journey?"

I see a flicker in Grandad's eyes. "The whale… it's coming," he says. He tries to speak again, but a sore groan comes from his lopsided mouth. He opens his hand.

Josh jumps back and falls over Linus's scooter, tearing his knees on the pavement. Megan gasps and backs away. Only Linus stays beside me and stares at the robin, at the ounce of lifeless feathers in Grandad's hands.

7.

"How long will Grandad be in hospital?" Jodie says that night.

It was a stroke that took a whole chunk more of Grandad away from us. The blood supply to his brain had been interrupted and more brain cells had died. It made the symptoms of Alzheimer's worse, like he'd jumped down a whole staircase instead of taking the disease step by step.

Mum shakes her head. "We don't know, love. He's going to need some help to get him back on his feet again."

"And then he's coming home," I say, "so that I can look after him."

Mum and Dad glance sideways at each other.

"We're not sure what the process is just yet," Dad says. "Grandad is going to need a lot of therapy over the next few months—"

"Months?" I ask. He can't be in hospital for months. I have to remind him of August 18th. I have to know what the story is so that we can go on our journey together.

"Weeks," Mum says, "it might only be weeks." Again she glances at Dad.

"Did Grandad say anything?" I ask. "Anything about me or anything at all?"

Mum shakes her head. "I don't know if he

knew it was me," she says quietly. "I don't think he recognised either of us."

I push between Mum and Dad on the sofa, the only space I can see that feels safe.

"Can we visit him?" Jodie says, squeezing on the other side of Mum.

"Not just yet," Dad says.

Mum touches Dad's arm. "He's very confused and weak at the moment," she says. "I'll go in tomorrow to check how he is and let you all know. Then we'll see when he's up to having more visitors."

We know that nobody gets better from Alzheimer's, but the doctor said it's possible Grandad can recover from some of the symptoms of the stroke. But the way Mum described him sounded all wrong, like it was someone else in hospital, not my grandad. I keep thinking he's still here, somewhere, only I can't find him.

I get up from the sofa.

"I don't want to see him in hospital," I say. "But when he comes home, there's something we have to do."

"What's that?" asks Dad.

They all look at me and I'm not sure now how to say what I'm thinking. Our journeys were about being together and discovering things, and seeing the world in front of us with bright eyes and open ears. I was going to take him out in the boat again. We wouldn't go far – we'd stay in the inlets and quiet harbour waters. Because I'm sure, if we did, he'd remember everything he wanted to tell me.

"We're going to take a journey together," I say, but don't wait for them to ask questions because I can't explain anything more. How can I tell them that I think we're going to find a whale?

I go out to the kitchen and rummage through the cupboards until I find the spray gun. I fill the bottle with cold water from the tap. I go out to the garden and shout into the night shadows, "Just you wait until Grandad gets back, Smokey! I know it was you that killed the robin."

8.

"Did you think something was wrong with Grandad yesterday morning?" Jodie says when I meet her on the quay the next day on the way home from school.

I feel guilty because I've been trying to cover up some of the things he did, and maybe I shouldn't have done that.

"Yes, but most of the time he was fine," I say.

It's an effort to lie and makes my stomach hurt. "I wanted him to be fine," I say quietly.

Jodie knows I feel bad and I can trust her not to make me feel worse.

We stare at the statue of the faceless people.

"It's weird how they didn't give them faces," Jodie says.

"Mrs Gooch said it's so we can all see something of ourselves in them."

Jodie pulls a face and I know what she's thinking. Nobody's faces are the same – they have different shapes and colours and ways that they are put together.

"It's not like a mirror or anything," I say. "It's just that it's supposed to remind us of things like being safe or rescued or people we know, something like that."

I see Grandad and me in the statue. He's the

big brave figure in the boat reaching for the small one, to carry them safely back to shore.

"What's the greatest power on earth, Jodie?"

"That sounds like something Grandad would say."

"It is something he said, ages ago. He was going to tell me a story... about a journey."

Jodie screws up her face and tips her head to the side. "Maybe the greatest power on earth is Art," she says, taking a long look at the statue. "But not this bit of art. It's weird."

I notice Jodie has black eyeliner and mascara and her lips are glossy and pink.

"Have you got a boyfriend?" I say.

"No!" she says, far too strongly.

"Thought so. You don't normally wear so much make-up. What's your boyfriend's name?"

"He's not my boyfriend," she says, "I just like him."

"How much?"

Jodie's painted eyes open wider.

"Loads," she says which makes us smile, but our faces drop again straight away. Even that can't stop us thinking about Grandad.

We walk along the quay to Hambourne slipway.

"Is this where you found Grandad?" Jodie says. I nod. "What was he doing here?"

Behind the slipway and across the other side of the road is a fairly new row of flats. I can't remember what was there before it became a building site, before they built the flats. I don't know if that has anything to do with why he came here.

Three red inflatable boats, with big engines on the back, are moored at the slipway. Divers are unpacking air tanks and crates on to the quayside. There's a journalist and a cameraman there and

66

they are interviewing another man nearby.

"I wonder what they've been doing," Jodie says.

"It must be important because they're filming it."

"Were the divers here yesterday? Maybe Grandad heard something about it on the radio and came to see."

I look up at Jodie. "I didn't notice."

"Maybe he was lost." Jodie sighs. "You must have been really scared."

I was, because of what might have happened. Grandad could have fallen in the sea. My lips tremble with the cold thought that things could have been even worse. And because she's Jodie she puts her arm out so I can snuggle in.

We watch the gulping tide below at the bottom of the steps and the three long red boats rocking as the divers take the equipment out. The sky is grey and it makes the sea grey and blank too and I wonder if that's what it's like for Grandad right now. Just looking at lots of the same nothing. I want to be with him, and I don't. I want to be with Grandad as he was before Alzheimer's took him away.

I try to listen to what the journalist is saying. I can't hear the man who's being interviewed, but he waves towards the harbour and then folds his arms and nods.

"We could ask *them*," Jodie says. "They might have seen Grandad here yesterday."

I shake my head. When someone has Alzheimer's, it feels like a private thing.

"Is your boyfriend from school?" I say to Jodie to change the subject because my eyes keep falling back on the greyness below us.

"He might be," Jodie smiles, and I know she

feels the same and would really rather talk about him, and it'll be much easier than what we're thinking about. "He's doing the Furze Island Project, so I'll get to see him most of the summer."

I pretend I have a microphone like the journalist and make it sound like I'm interviewing her.

"Today, I'm talking to a girl called Jodie Gray who is fifteen and is wearing lipgloss and she's going to tell us lots of interesting things. So, Jodie, what's the Furze Island Project?"

Jodie coughs and smile, as if there really is a camera filming her, and puts on a newsreader's voice.

"The Furze Island Project is run by a group of volunteers from our school. You have to be in Year Ten or Eleven and enjoy being outdoors and interested in nature conservation. The volunteers are going to clean the beach and clear some gorse, and look out for wildlife and make a record of what's there."

"Very interesting," I say, thinking of another question. "And is it just girls or are there boys doing it as well?"

Jodie gives me a look. "Both." Then she twinkles, "Including a very handsome boy called Adam."

I notice Jodie's cheeks don't need blusher because they're pink anyway.

"I think you love Adam," I say.

"Hannah!" Jodie says, nudging me. I make my voice deeper and more serious.

"Thank you, Jodie," I say. I hold out the pretend microphone to her again. "And what sort of wildlife are you looking for?"

"Any," she says. "Whatever we see we'll make a record of, but we've especially got to keep an eye out for red squirrels, lizards, whales—"

"Whales?" I say, startled.

She shrugs. "Or dolphins, anything unusual."

"No, but you said whales."

"I know. *Whales* – what's wrong with saying that?" Jodie has her shoulders up and her palms turned out like I'm being silly. "We won't see whales, they don't come here. I'm just saying that's what I was told to look out for. *Anything*, including whales."

I reach back in time, and I hear Grandad telling me, *Let's see if we can find that whale*.

I wish I'd not gone to school yesterday because then maybe he wouldn't have had the stroke, I could have kept him safe. Imagining these things makes my mouth dry. I am breathing too fast.

"Where *can* you find whales?"

Jodie shakes her head. "What do you mean?"

71

"Think," I say. "Where could Grandad have gone and seen a whale?"

She shrugs. "Why? What's wrong?"

"I think we were going on a journey in the summer holidays. He said something about a whale. Just before he had the stroke… he said to remember August the eighteenth for him." I try to take a deep breath because all of a sudden I can't remember how to breathe and my lungs won't fill. "I should have stayed at home with him."

Jodie curls her arm round me again. She whispers, "Shh, it's not your fault; nobody expects you to look after him," and then a long minute passes before my lungs remember what to do.

"Can we go home now?" I say. "I need to find out everything I can about whales for when Grandad comes out of hospital."

I'm going to look on the computer to see if I can work out where Grandad wants to take me. And, if Grandad can't tell me what's important, I'll find out for myself.

9.

W<small>HEN</small> M<small>UM</small> <small>COMES</small> <small>HOME,</small> <small>SHE</small> <small>SAYS,</small> "W<small>HAT</small> <small>ARE</small> you doing here all by yourself, Hannah? Where's Jodie, she's supposed to stay with you after school?"

"She had to meet up with her friends from the Furze Island Project."

Mum looks around at the floor. She crouches beside me and holds my shoulders.

"What have you been doing?" she says.

Memories of the past are still circling in my mind, the things that Grandad had said: *Remember August the eighteenth for me*; the night I'd been sick when he talked of Grandma, *Something great put us together, bound us together forever, and it will never be undone*; in the boat when we saw the deer, *Will you stay or will you swim across?*; yesterday morning, *Let's see if we can find that whale.*

I'm shocked at what I now see around me, the mess I've left from searching through cupboards and drawers, through old papers and photographs and passports. I thought I'd find something from Grandad's past that I could hold on to until he came home, something real in my hands, because I can't think of a place in the future where Grandad and I can be together.

"I've been looking for a whale."

10.

At dinnertime I give Dad a list of countries where you can see a whale. He keeps chewing and slides the piece of paper across to Mum. "I don't think Grandad's ever been on an aeroplane," he says. "I don't see how he could have gone to any of these places."

"He didn't come with us when we went on holiday to Spain either," Mum says. "What about Scotland?"

Dad doesn't look convinced. "When did he go to Scotland? Grandad's not been much of a traveller."

"It's probably a memory from when he was young," I say. People with Alzheimer's often remember things from a long time ago.

I realise none of us could have known him then. Nobody can think of anything. We are blank and useless. He must have gone somewhere to see a whale before. Why else would he say we were going to find one?

"What's the greatest power on earth?" I ask.

"Do you mean like volcanoes or earthquakes?" Dad says.

"Maybe, I don't know."

"Is this something Grandad said?" Mum asks. "One of his big ideas?"

I nod.

"What about family bonds?" Mum suggests.

I like that, but then I feel the heaviness in my stomach because of who is missing. I'm not sure what it has to do with a whale though.

Just then Jodie bursts in through the front door, takes her plate out of the oven and comes to the table. She starts eating before she's taken off her jacket or sat down.

"What?" she says because Dad is staring at her.

"You were supposed to be here with Hannah," Dad says.

Jodie draws a sharp breath. "I forgot!"

"Forgot?" Dad says, shaking his head, which makes us all think again.

"Look, we're relying on you—" Dad begins.

"I know, I know," Jodie interrupts. "I'm sorry, I won't do it again."

Mum raises her eyebrows at Jodie, but I'm thinking it's not fair to blame her.

"I'll remind her," I say.

Jodie looks at me while she's trying to eat and take her jacket off at the same time. "Guess what?"

Dad tells her to sit down properly.

"Have you found out something about a whale?" I ask.

She hesitates, the fork near her mouth, and blinks slowly.

"No, but you know those divers we saw earlier, Hannah?" she says. "They've found something on the harbour seabed."

I put down my knife and fork. I wonder what they've found.

11.

THREE WEEKS PASS BEFORE MUM AND DAD SAY
Grandad is ready for Jodie and me to visit. I still
don't want to go. I don't want to see him until
he's better and back with us. And I'm scared of
what I'll find in the hospital bed. A grandad who
doesn't know us.

I write a kind of diary for Grandad while I'm
afraid to go and see him, while I wait for him to

come back home. I tell him about the birds and the sunflowers. I try to make all the good things sound bigger than they are, but it's hard to find anything that stands out without him here. I don't say that I think Smokey's been again, that there are fewer sparrows than before.

I tell Mum and Dad that I have to revise for a test at school and they don't question why we're having a test right at the end of term, but drop me off at Megan's instead.

Megan talks non-stop about the summer holidays and going to Tenerife. She talks about her new swimming costume and sunglasses and other small things.

I ask her what she knows about whales. She shrugs. "They're big," she says. I still haven't told any of my friends that Grandad has Alzheimer's. I don't think they'll understand. We both avoid talking about what happened to Grandad near Hambourne slipway, but I ask her if she knows what used to be there, before they built the new flats. She can't remember either. I don't think it's just Alzheimer's that makes people forget.

I decide that when Grandad comes home I'll have to wait for the moments when he is bright and here with us. I'll wait for the ocean of nothing to clear from his eyes and we'll plan our journey to find a whale. I need something to look forward to.

Dad, Mum and Jodie pick me up after their visit to the hospital.

"Is he better?" I ask.

I see in Jodie's face that she's disappointed, like she'd arranged to meet someone and they weren't there. I think she's hoped too much, but now she's giving up. "He didn't know me," she says.

I stretch the seat belt out and lean forward.

"He has to come home, doesn't he, Mum?" I say. "And then he'll have all the familiar things around him. That will help him remember us."

We pull up outside our house. Nobody undoes their seat belt or gets out. Mum touches Dad's arm as if to stop him from speaking.

"She needs to know," he says.

There is an ocean of silence before Dad's words smack through the air.

"Grandad isn't coming home."

"What do you mean?"

"He's being moved into a unit where they can look after him."

"A unit? What's a unit?" I hear the shriek in my voice. I hadn't meant it to come out like that just as Dad hadn't meant to hurt me with what he said.

"It's a care home," Mum says, frowning at Dad.

"A place where they specialise in looking after people with Alzheimer's disease."

"How long?" I say.

"It's the best place for him," Dad says. This time Dad reaches for Mum's hand. "We all agreed."

"Home is the best place for him," I say. "How long?"

"We're sorry, Hannah," Dad says, "but he's going to stay there now for good."

No. I can't believe that they have made that decision for Grandad. How could they? I slam the car door and run through the house, straight to the back door. Smokey, the thieving cat, is sitting on our lawn. I creep out of the back door and turn on the tap and point the hosepipe at him.

"You're the one that's not wanted here!" I yell.

Smokey leaps up on to the fence, but when I follow him with the spray the water stops to a dribble. Dad has turned the tap off.

Mum follows Dad into the garden. She takes the hose from me.

"There is something we can do," Mum says. "The people we saw from the care home said we should try to bring some memories from home to take to him, especially things from his past."

"Come here," Dad says and wraps me into his belly. "I'm sorry I had to tell you. We all need to know where we are."

But I feel more lost than ever.

12.

Eᴀꜱᴛ Hᴀʀʙᴏᴜʀ Cᴀʀᴇ Hᴏᴍᴇ ɪꜱ ᴀ ᴡɪᴅᴇ ʙᴜɪʟᴅɪɴɢ up on a cliff with a view out to sea. I go with the family to visit Grandad when he's been moved there. But it's not like our home. It smells of disinfectant and mashed potato. We wait at reception and I look back through the doors. At least he can see the sea from here.

We pass other rooms in the hallway; they

all have the same carpet and furniture, new and plain, as if somebody furnished this place without thinking how different all the people would be.

Grandad's outside is familiar, his tall broad shoulders, his long legs, his wide sandpaper hands. But the more his memory vanishes, the more something inside of him shrinks as well. It's as if all of his unique Grandad-ness has been stolen right out of his body by the stroke, as if whatever held him together before is crumbling. He's sitting differently; his shoulders curve and sag. I don't think he can sit upright because he's tall and it's not his chair with the soft bow in the seat and the high back and the varnish wearing off the arms. There's nothing of us here either, none of our furniture or our things.

"Hello, Grandad," I say and it's hard saying those words because I don't want to feel like a visitor, someone who calls in now and then.

He doesn't recognise me.

I give him a bar of chocolate, but he seems to have forgotten the sweetness of that too. I want him to know that I didn't agree to him being here. Mum and Dad made that decision. But I don't know how to tell him so he'll remember. What if he only keeps a memory of us abandoning him?

"It's me, Hannah." My voice wobbles. "Your grandaughter." It's like I have to start all over again with him.

"He's trying to remember," Mum says, "and you know that if he possibly could, he'd find a way."

Dad reads the newspaper out loud, but Grandad doesn't seem interested. The diary isn't working; neither do the old photographs that Mum shows him. She's brought in a framed family photo of us all, but there's nowhere to hang it. Dad says he'll have a word about that. I try and find somewhere for it to lean, but there are gaps between the furniture and walls, and no space on the surfaces, so I have to put it in a drawer and that nearly takes all my breath away again so I leave the drawer open.

There has to be another way to help him.

I kneel down and put my hand on Grandad's knee and wait for him to pile his hands over mine. His eyes brighten and I know he feels me touch him, but his hands stay where they are.

"Grandad?" I say. "I had a rubbish day at school."

Every day after school, Grandad used to ask me to tell him what had happened that day. Sometimes it was what I learned in geography or history, sometimes it was about my friends or other people, sometimes things I liked, what annoyed me or made me sad, or things I was afraid of. Grandad's beard would crackle as he rubbed his chin and listened. It was like pouring out my day and giving it to him. If things made me unhappy, he'd always ask me to look at things another way.

"I got in a mood with Megan because she was talking about going on holiday and I'm not going anywhere." Megan's holiday reminded me that Grandad and I wouldn't be able to take a journey together now.

I wait for him to ask his brilliant big questions that make all the bad things sound small and insignificant, for the horrible feelings to vanish, for all the good things to shine.

"Grandad?" I ask him again to come back to us. "It's all rubbish without you."

It's strange how our memories suddenly bring us something. I remember him saying, *You have* to think big, Hannah, and when things are good, think bigger.

I don't know what happens then, but when I look up for a moment I see Grandad as I always used to. He is still a giant in my memory. I feel him sheltering me, like he always has. He must still be here. And if he is then we must also be in there somewhere.

And then I think, *what if I take the journey on my own and find the whale for him?*

13.

THE HOLIDAYS BEGIN. IN THE SUMMER SEASON tourists come to Hambourne, to the pottery gift shop that Mum and Dad open for long hours near the quay. Mum tells Jodie she will have to look after me because neither Mum nor Dad can take time off. She says that some people think it's a burden having old folk around, but Grandad had made life easier for everyone.

"But I'll be doing the Furze Island Project from next week," Jodie sulks.

"You'll have to apologise and pull out," Mum says.

"But I'm going to be with my friends!"

She thinks that's a good enough reason, but Mum and Dad have told her often, like Mum does now, "The world doesn't revolve around your social life, Jodie."

"She wants to be with Adam," I say.

"Who's Adam?" Mum says.

Jodie drops her shoulders and makes a big huffy sigh. "Nobody," she says, glaring at me.

"Well, he must be somebody," Mum says.

"He's doing the Furze Island Project," Jodie says through her teeth. "And I want to do it too!"

Mum sighs; she wants the argument over.

"Do you remember when we went to Furze

Island, Hannah?" Mum says. "Grandad was with us."

"Me?" I say, but I don't remember. Furze Island is in the middle of the harbour and is only open to tourists for the sunny months of the year.

"I'm not sure where Jodie was that day," Mum says.

"Why haven't we been back?" I say.

Mum shakes her head and shrugs. "Too busy working probably."

It's funny how we hardly ever seem to visit some of the things on our doorstep. They're so familiar and, even though I can see the island every day from our garden or Grandad's bedroom, I hardly notice that it's there at all.

"Mum?" Jodie says. "We were discussing me!"

Maybe it's because I've seen those journalists and cameramen recently, but I think about making a film. I think of recording the things that Grandad has shared with us in his life, something that will help him remember us when he watches it.

"Why don't I go with Jodie instead?" I say.

Mum raises her eyebrows. "Now that sounds like a good plan. Jodie?"

"But, Mum!" Jodie whines.

"Jodie, would you just do as you're asked for a change? If Grandad was well then Hannah could stay at home, but you know Dad and I have to work and you need to do your fair share."

Any time Jodie gets in a mood Mum and Dad remind her that Grandad is the reason we should stop arguing. It makes everything sound like it's Grandad's fault though.

"Could we buy a video camera?" I ask. "I want to make a film for Grandad of all the places he's been. Where exactly did we go on the island?"

"I haven't agreed," Jodie huffs.

Mum ignores her. "South Beach or was it East Beach?" Her eyes close, her forehead wrinkles. "I remember him talking about the deer that live there."

"What about the deer?" Last year, when Grandad and I had been out in the boat and saw the fawn and the deer, he'd talked as if they had a history together. I don't know how to put all the pieces together, but I'm sure the deer have something to do with the story he wanted to tell me. "Mum, what did he say?"

"Let me think…"

I squeeze her hands between mine. "Mum, you have to remember. It could be very, very important."

14.

I MAKE HER A CUP OF TEA AND SIT WITH MUM ON
the sofa.

"I'm not sure what I remember," Mum says.
"It was quite a few years ago."

"Mum, pretend I'm doing an interview and I'll
ask questions. Maybe that will help you."

"OK," she says and leans back. "Ask away."

"When did we go?"

She takes a moment, breathes a long breath through her nose and closes her eyes.

"You would have been about eighteen months old, so it was probably near the end of the summer holidays."

"Was it sunny?"

She hesitates. "Yes, warm and breezy."

"And we went on the ferry from the quay?"

"Yes. Oh yes, and we took a picnic with us... and a blanket... and a bucket and spade, for you. You were wearing flip-flops and they wouldn't stay on your feet. Grandad carried you and the buggy..." She turns her head to me and opens her eyes. I know she sees Grandad as he was. "I'm always nervous crossing the gangplank and he was so much stronger back then." I nod. "And you... you've never seemed to be afraid of anything when you're around him." I smile;

98

I'm enjoying a memory of him.

I remember being in my cot, waking early, dawn breaking through the curtains. I stood up and rattled the bars and yelled for Grandad. I heard soft footsteps in the hall, the click of the door handle. I held out my arms, then I was up near the ceiling with Grandad. No, I never felt afraid around him.

Mum's smiling. We turn on our sides so we're facing each other.

"Where did we go when we got to the island, Mum?"

"South Beach. Down the steps. Grandad was still carrying you. We had our picnic."

"And then?"

"I think I lay there. Maybe snoozed… no, I read a book and you went paddling with Grandad. That's right. He carried you a long way out to sea.

I could hear you crying and he waved for me to come out."

"Did you?"

"I hitched up my skirt and waded out!" She laughs and it's nice because I can almost feel like I'm there too. "The water was only up to my knees, but I felt like I'd walked for a mile."

"Why was I crying?"

"I don't know." She's quiet for a moment. "I don't think you cried for long." She kisses me. "Grandad was talking to you while you were out there, telling you something that made you stop crying. You see, I've never had to worry about you. Not with Grandad around."

I wonder what he'd said. He always knew what to say to make me feel better.

"What about the deer, Mum? What did he say about them?"

She closes her eyes again. "The deer?" I hear her breath. "He was talking about Grandma." Her eyes open. "Actually, I think she was probably the one who had a soft spot for the deer. Yes, I remember now. I think something happened to the deer during World War Two and it took a while for the population to recover. I think he said they used to go out in the boat to check on them. I never saw them go though."

"Did they go to Gorbreen or Furze Island?"

She frowns then shrugs. "You know, even when they were getting old, your grandparents were still like a couple of kids. Secretive and very sweet to each other. "

"They never took you with them?"

"No. I suppose it was just something they did together."

"I wish I'd known Grandma."

"Yes, I wish you had too."

It's quiet for a moment and I can tell she's thinking about Grandma because her eyes and smile are soft.

"Mum, did Grandad ever tell you a special story about the deer or maybe about one important deer?"

"No, he didn't."

I roll on to my back. I think I've found a path back to Grandad, but I'm not sure what it means at all. Alzheimer's is taking his memory away, but maybe I can find lots of clues to remind him.

"Mum? Grandad said he was saving a story to tell me." I don't know how to say the next bit, but Mum has already worked it out.

"You mean why didn't he tell me?" She's smiling and it's OK. "That's simple. He always had Grandma before you came along."

Jodie comes in and sits between us and I can tell by the way she cuddles us both that she's been listening.

"All right," Jodie says. "Maybe I will let you come to the island with me, Hannah."

"And maybe," I say, "maybe we'll find a whale too."

15.

We don't have the money for a video camera so Dad borrows an old one from someone he knows. Dad's a bit funny about money at the moment because he says it's taking a while to sort out Grandad's savings to pay for him to be at the care home.

Jodie and I have a couple of days at home before we go to Furze Island and I try to think of the best way to film things. I want this to be special, to be just for Grandad.

Jodie helps me tape the camera to Dad's hard hat, so that the camera is just above my eyes. Only the hat is too big and I have to keep pushing up the peak.

"Do I look stupid?" I say.

"I've spent ages doing this," Jodie says. "So, no."

When I walk out of the house, Linus and Josh are sitting on our wall. I haven't seen them for a while.

"Why are you wearing a hard hat?" Linus says.

Josh looks up. "Is it raining frogs?"

And I have to say, "No, silly. I'm making a film."

They inspect the camera and Josh smirks and says, "Your film's not going to be very interesting."

He crouches in front of me and looks up and waves and makes silly voices. Linus looks at my face and yanks Josh up by his T-shirt.

Josh says, "What?"

But Linus ignores him and says, "Do you want to borrow my scooter, Hannah?"

I grit my teeth because actually I want to punch Josh because I don't like someone making fun of something important I'm trying to do. But instead I look at Linus and say, "What for?"

"Dunno," he shrugs. "Maybe you could put the camera on it."

"Then you could film people's ankles," Josh giggles.

"Shut up, Josh," says Linus.

"Yeah, shut up," I say and go back inside the house.

Jodie and I watch the film back and realise

why Josh had said it wasn't very interesting. The camera had slipped and I'd recorded my shoes and the pavement, and then Linus's and Josh's shoes and the pavement, and then Josh crouched there making stupid voices and noises, which is extremely dull and annoying. So it hasn't really worked.

I have another think. Jodie helps me strap the camera with strong tape to an old baby harness round my chest. It feels right, like I'll be recording things from my heart, which seems better than the one cold eye of the camera.

"Does *this* look stupid as well?" I say.

"No," Jodie says, "not really."

Then we realise we've put the lens cap somewhere and can't find it, but Jodie says, "Just use this when you've finished," which is a clean milk bottle top and some more tape.

I'm recording all our everyday things, trying to make all the solid things in our house seem as real on a screen to Grandad. I hope his eyes will be able to see more.

Jodie makes us lunch and afterwards we sit down to watch the recording of our house from my heart, and this is what we watch: boring cupboards in the kitchen and then my food on the plate and pieces of sausage disappearing over the top of the camera. And then we watch Jodie getting up from the other side of the table because she has finished her lunch, only you wouldn't know it was her because it is just her middle and then her back.

"What's that in my pocket?" Jodie says because we see the outline of something circular as she disappears off the screen.

Jodie feels in her back pocket. The lens cap!

It makes me think about how the film shows us something from a bit earlier, something we hadn't noticed at the time. And I wonder if you watched your whole day back, would you find all sorts of things?

Then we watch beans being pushed around with a knife and fork, and then the plate is carried into the kitchen and the beans scraped and we see them plop into the bin.

Jodie says, "I didn't see you do that earlier."

So I tell her the beans were nice, but there were too many, and remind her that my stomach is actually very small because it's in proportion to the rest of me.

"I know," she says. "I didn't think I gave you too much."

And then in the film I go over and put my plate in the sink and the picture goes black and the sound is muffled for ages because I was leaning against the sink and washing up.

"It's not right," I say. "It's not the sort of film I want."

"No," Jodie says. "But it's us doing ordinary things and that's important for Grandad."

I thought it would be easy to make a film, but it isn't. And it's hard to find things that stick out big and bright, full of the wonders we saw every day. It isn't like how I remember things with Grandad.

"I thought the film would be about us, but we're hardly in it at all," I say.

"Maybe you should just hold the camera instead," Jodie sighs. She is already bored.

The phone rings. One of Jodie's friends. She sits cross-legged on the floor and flicks through a magazine while she talks.

I put the harness back on.

"I'm going out," I say. Jodie waves, but she's had enough now. "If I see Josh again and he says anything about me wearing a baby harness, I'm going to poke his eyes out." Jodie isn't listening. "And if he laughs I'm going to kick his shins." She nods.

I roll my eyes at her. "What?" she mouths.

"Nothing."

I go outside to look for the birds. I try to fill the film with the things that might remind Grandad of us. Maybe then he'll find us too.

16.

Today I'm up in Grandad's bedroom trying something else. I'm pointing the camera through Grandad's binoculars, which makes a circle on the film like a telescope, and I quite like that. I film the grey-green sea and Furze Island in the harbour and plenty of sky and the buildings and boats that look like toys from here.

Closer to our house I hear *clip*, *clip*, *clip* and

point the camera at Mr Howard who is cutting his hedge and a lady walking past with her dog that looks anxious and yaps at him. And then the dog jumps to the side and barks as something silver flashes past. I've zoomed in too much and can't tell what it is at first. I follow the silver flash and see Linus on the other side of the road with his scooter and he's looking up at me.

"Are you going to be making a film today?" he shouts.

"I might be," I say. "Where's Josh?"

"What?" he says.

I realise I can hear him through the glass, but he can't hear me and I wonder why that is. I think about shouting louder, but it's no use.

"Come out," Linus says, squinting up at me. "I can't hear you."

Jodie is leaning over the kitchen counter,

talking on the telephone.

"I'm going out filming with Linus," I say.

She nods and puts her hand over the phone and mouths, "Don't go far."

When I get outside, Linus sees the camera strapped to the toddler harness. I put my hands on my hips to dare him to say anything. But he doesn't laugh.

"I know it's a baby harness," I say, just in case.

"You never know when one of those things might come in handy," he says. "You've practically invented something new though."

"Where's Josh?"

"He had to stay home and tidy his room because they've got family coming for a barbecue this afternoon," Linus says. "It's just me. Where's Megan?"

"Abroad on holiday," I sigh.

Then he hands over his scooter and says, "Do you want to film from the scooter?"

Linus jogs across the road and waves to make me follow him. He runs backwards, calling, "You can go really fast down Southbrook Hill."

I've already pressed play on the camera and am kicking my right foot against the pavement to catch him up.

At the bottom of Southbrook Hill we sit on the pavement with our backs against somebody's garden wall and play the film back on the small screen. Linus pushes his nest of curly hair away from his face because he's sweaty from running.

"It's good," he says. "Like an action film."

And it is good. Because the pavement and houses and everything either side are whizzing past, as if we'd stayed very still and it all rolled towards us. We hear the rattle of the scooter

against the road and Linus's footsteps running and sometimes his legs kick into the picture and sometimes they don't. And there's a blustery noise of the wind against the microphone that suddenly goes quiet when we stop at the bottom, and I don't know why but I like that.

I'm not in the film again, but it makes me think of something.

Before I play it again I say to Linus, "Pretend you don't know I was filming it and it's the first time you've seen it and you're not allowed to think that it's me on the scooter and you running. Pretend you don't know anything and watch it again."

And I can see by the way he shakes back his curly fringe that he's getting ready to do it. Linus leans right in as if he's looking for something hidden in the film that he didn't see before. That's why I like Linus. He wouldn't mind looking at a caterpillar on the playing field at school even if all the other boys are having a game of football.

I press play and we see and hear it all again: the whizzing street, the rattle, the footsteps, the blustering and then the stopping.

"Well?" I say because he isn't saying anything. "Did you pretend, like I said?"

And I don't want to tell him what to say. It's no good thinking something extraordinary if nobody else thinks it. He shrugs.

"Never mind," I say. "I'm just practising things at the moment. But I think the scooter is a good idea because it makes the camera steadier than when I'm walking."

Then Linus says, "Well, it's kind of like anyone could watch it and think it's them running or on the scooter."

That's what I'm thinking too, about Grandad as a boy, of his childhood memories. People with Alzheimer's seem to remember things from long ago. Maybe if he watched a film like this he'd remember being a boy.

I give Linus my best smile.

"Is the film for your grandad?" he says.

I nod.

"Thought so," Linus says. His hair falls over his eyes, but I see him. "My nan had Alzheimer's; we made a photo album for her and took her roses because they were her favourite. I was too young to think of making a film."

I didn't realise he knew about Grandad. I didn't know about his nan either. I'm sad for him, but it's nice knowing I'm not the only one.

We sit together for a minute, thinking of our own grandparents and memories.

"Thanks for trying to help me with Grandad," I say. Linus shrugs. "Linus?"

"What?"

"Do you know where I can find a whale?"

"Yeah."

"You do?"

"Well, not *find* it exactly. I saw one on a nature programme."

"Oh.

"Linus? What do you think is the greatest power on earth?"

"Probably a space rocket because it has to get through the atmosphere. What do you think?"

"I think…" I'm thinking it's probably something like your memory, but I don't say it. "I think I should be in the film too."

I rip off the tape and harness and give the camera to Linus. He points it at me and I talk.

"Grandad, it's me, Hannah. We were supposed to be going on a journey together, but…" Then I tell Linus to stop filming. Every time I think about the future I feel afraid, like something is crumbling inside me and I can't hold on to it. Grandad's not coming home. He's not going anywhere with me.

I'm ten – how am I supposed to make the journey on my own? I don't even know where I'm supposed to go.

17.

THE YELLOW FERRY IS THE BRIGHTEST THING ON the quay. But it isn't the only bright thing. The sun is shining on the green tiles of the Anchor Inn, and sparkling on the choppy waves and catching the white bellies of the gulls that are spinning round the chinking masts.

The gulls laugh and the air tastes of salt and vinegar on chips.

Everything looks like it's made of white and yellow sunlight and I film it all. I wonder if it's the same as when Grandad was a boy.

The harbour is huge, one of the biggest in the world, with lots of inlets further inland where Grandad and I have explored from Gorbreen. Furze Island is in the middle of the harbour like a green roundabout in the motorway sea. That's where I'm going with Jodie. It takes about twenty minutes to walk across the island from east to west, and about half the time across the middle. There are a few stone cottages and a shop, but not many people live there. There are no cars and all the criss-crossing paths are for walking around the island or leading you down to the beach. It's for wildlife really.

There are eleven other teenagers mooching around the yellow sign by the ferry when Jodie and I go over. The girls are huddled together and the boys are in a row near them. Straight away I know which boy is Adam. He's the one that makes Jodie fidgety and twist her hoop earrings when he stands next to her.

When Jodie says she had to bring her little sister with her, Adam says, "Hey, squirt, you could be our camera girl."

Jodie goes pink because Adam leans on her arm, but I don't like that he called me squirt!

"Hannah, actually," I say, as tough as I can. "It's a palindrome, which means it's the same spelled forwards as it is backwards."

Adam laughs. "What do you say, do you want to do some filming for us… Hannah the palindrome?"

"Maybe," I say.

I suppose he's all right because he doesn't leave

me out and it makes Jodie glad that I'm there. Sort of.

"Hey, Jode," Adam says. I widen my eyes at her, but she doesn't say anything even though she wouldn't normally like anyone calling her *Jode*. "Hannah could record some of the things we'll be doing, you know, like a before and after thing so we can document the project."

"Yeah, great idea, Adam," she exaggerates, like it's the cleverest thing she's ever heard. She thinks *I'm* embarrassing.

It's nice then because Jodie can be more normal with me like she is at home and doesn't have to act like she's been lumbered with her little sister.

Jodie and her friends are excited about what they're going to be doing and suddenly everyone is talking and talking as we board the ferry. They're too busy to notice the little sailing boats banking in the breeze, or that the white clouds are flat on the bottom and bubbly on the top and seem to be queuing to come in from over the sea. That's what I film. I lean over the side of the ferry and point the camera at the bow breaking the waves. Jodie grabs my jacket tight so I don't fall in and I notice that her group have moved away and all the girls are gathered round Adam.

The breeze is strong when we get off the boat. People struggle against it as it bustles them along the gangway, as it snatches at their clothes. I feel the breeze swooping along the harbour wall, pushing into our backs like soft, salty hands.

A man and lady are waiting at the Furze Island visitor centre and they talk for a bit and then put the volunteers into two groups and Jodie tells me to just keep quiet. I follow Jodie and her group across the island and sit at the bottom of the steps that lead down to the beach while they turn right and spread out with their rubbish bags.

This is South Beach, where Grandad and Mum and I came once.

I film the crushed flint and shells crackling under my feet and the surf sizzling and scalloping on the sand like lace. I zoom in and film an oystercatcher skimming the waves. I talk as if I remember, but I don't. I say, "Remember, Grandad? We came here one day."

Just then a laughing face with brown floppy hair comes up close in the picture and waves. It's Adam and he holds up his black bag and says he's found two plastic bottles already and a piece of driftwood. His voice gets carried away in the sea breeze. He runs along the beach with the wind, over to Jodie who's found some fishing line tangled in seaweed.

Adam shows Jodie the pale cracked driftwood and he turns it over and points at something. Normally people find special things for themselves on the beach, like shells and smooth pebbles with spying holes. I think Adam must really like Jodie because he gives his special piece of wood to her.

I take off my sandals and walk out into the shallow water and keep filming. I walk a long way, but the water only comes up to my knees. I say out loud, "Grandad, remember you walked me out in the sea? You told me something when I was too small to remember, but you made me stop crying."

The divers with red inflatable boats that I'd seen at Hambourne slipway are out in the deep channel of the harbour. There are other boats there too and another much bigger boat with a crane moored alongside them. The picture blurs the closer I zoom in, but I can see the divers in the water.

"They've found a wreck or something buried on the seabed, Grandad. It was on the news. One of those planes that takes photographs of the ground saw a long dark shape in the water and took a picture of it. They're not sure what it is yet though."

The divers are waving their arms, like they're telling the others to stop.

"They've got a crane, so it must be big, Grandad. Maybe they need something stronger to pull it up."

I stop, turn round, scan the coastline of the mainland and look back out to the channel.

Grandad had said that some journeys are over long distances. Some are closer to home.

It can't be deer or a whale, but I wonder if what they've found on the seabed could be the same as what I'm looking for.

18.

South Beach, Furze Island, again. This time Jodie and the others have turned on to a shorter section of the beach. There is a barbed-wire fence saying Keep Out so people can't go around to East Beach because the cliff is crumbling there. I film again. From this end of the beach I zoom the camera to the harbour entrance between the curves of the land, where the chain ferry crosses from one side to the other.

The deep water swirls and sucks and tugs at the boats. Sails stretch and boats lean into the wind. Beyond there I can see a little of the open sea that's like polished green glass. I wonder if Grandad ever rowed out there, but I need to find some more paths, some more clues about deer or whales.

At lunchtime Jodie, Adam and I sit on the beach with ham sandwiches, flapjacks and bottles of lemonade.

Adam goes down to the sea and throws some skimmers. Showing off.

"How's the filming going?" Jodie says.

"It's OK," I say. "I'm doing a journey kind of thing. But I need more things to film. I haven't got anything about deer or a whale yet."

"Adam's got something to tell you," Jodie says,

looking pleased with herself, and calls him over.

"Jodie told me you wanted to know about whales. I've already researched some stuff about them," Adam says. He winks at Jodie.

"Did you know that a humpback whale's heart is so big you could climb inside it?"

"Is it really?" I say.

"About as big as a car," Adam says.

I think of Grandad immediately. "Do you think having a big heart means you can love... bigger?"

Jodie blushes, but Adam doesn't look at her. "Whales' eyes are bigger than apples," he continues, "and they can blow water out of their blowholes about four metres high, maybe more."

And of course that means we have to try with our lemonade, making lemony spray out of our mouths. We laugh and Adam makes the tallest spray so Jodie thinks that is something worth liking about him even more. I run in the sea and swirl the fizz in my mouth and lose some in the breeze. It doesn't matter, Jodie says, when I worry about my clothes. It doesn't matter at all.

And then, right there in front of me, a long smooth curve rises out of the harbour waters. I swallow the lemonade as the dark shape surfaces.

"Look!" I shout. "Quick, look, Jodie! There's a whale!" Jodie and Adam stand up to see, as the tide falls away from the hump. It's gone for a few seconds and then emerges again as if something huge is swimming just below the surface. "It is, it is!"

I run back and turn the camera on, trying to steady the camera and myself. I zoom in, bring the dark shape closer and closer in the picture. "Grandad said it was coming!" I don't care why, I just think that if I can film it, if I can show

Grandad, then he'll remember the story. He'll remember the deer and it will all make sense.

Jodie touches my shoulder. "Look properly," she says.

I can see now. The falling tide has exposed a muddy sandbar.

"You couldn't get a whale in here," says Adam. The harbour's too shallow and they wouldn't be able to get past the chain ferry anyway."

"Don't say that," I say.

Jodie nudges Adam. "Sorry," he says. "It's true though."

He doesn't know everything, but he can make someone go from being high to down in the dumps in two seconds flat. I see Jodie widen her eyes at Adam.

"They have been seen once or twice off the south coast before though, Hannah," Adam says.

"There was actually one on the news the other night."

I'm burning Adam with my eyes because I don't want to speak to him, but I want to hear more.

Jodie speaks for me; she sounds irritated and I'm not sure why. "Why didn't you say?"

"It's hundreds of miles away, east, out in the English Channel."

"Grandad might have seen one there a long time ago," Jodie says for me. "Sometimes they go off course, or turn up in unexpected places."

"Jodie, can we go there?" I say.

And then she tells me all the reasons why we can't: It's too far; she's got the project to do; Dad and Mum won't agree; what will we do when we get there? Exactly where is it that I'm suggesting we go?

I walk to the shoreline, crouch down and film

the waves pulling away from me. The tide is going out and my feet are sinking in the sand, just like my hope is.

19.

I'M GETTING BORED. BORED WITH FILMING THE SAME seabirds and Adam and Jodie and the seashore and the nothing that's out there but salty water.

Jodie and Adam are making a chart of seabirds that they've seen and I've decided I don't like him that much any more. I'm moaning like Jodie does. "We're not going to see a whale here so I want to film deer," I say. "There's none down here though."

But now Jodie's in a mood. She says it's tough, she's busy, find something else to do. But time is running out. August 18th is less than a few weeks away. It's still a mystery what all these things have to do with what Grandad wanted to tell me. I'm more desperate than ever. I need to find enough things to show Grandad, so he'll remember.

I wade out into the water again, but I'm still seeing the same sea. Then I get a funny feeling, just like before when they unveiled the faceless statue, that someone is standing behind me.

I look up, scan along the East Beach. There's what looks like an old boathouse on the corner of the cliff, overgrown with ferns. I look up to the cliff top, about ten metres above us. An old lady is standing there in a gap where a high brick wall has fallen down. I think she's looking right at me. I turn from side to side, to see what else she might be looking at, but when I look up again she's still staring at me. She must live here. Maybe she knows where to find the deer. She must see everything from up there.

"Jodie," I whine, thinking if I get on her nerves she'll agree to anything. "I want to walk up to the cliff top, but I'm not supposed to be on my own."

Jodie's eyes are wide, her lips tight, and she's trying not to get cross in front of Adam. "Just make sure you meet me at the quay for the ferry," she whispers, flicking her head towards Adam. "I won't tell if you don't."

"I won't," I say. Inside I'm smiling. She's very easy to get round if it means she can be with Adam on her own.

I go up the steps and follow the path along the cliff top until the gorse is so thick I can't get through. I hear rustling in the spiny shadows. I creep away from the cliff to stalk round the bushes. There's a wall behind the overgrown gorse and bracken. I can see the roof of a house and palm trees spiking high into the sky. I find a gate that's open, just wide enough for a big cat to go through. Gorse has grown behind it too so it won't open any wider. There's a garden, crazy with rubble and wildness.

The old lady from the cliff top is now stooped in the middle of the garden, a dark silhouette with the sun behind her. She is wearing a crumpled straw hat and leaning on a stick. She's holding out her hand, feeding a deer. I knew it!

I turn the camera on, take a step, but as I force back the gate the crackling gorse startles the deer and it skitters through the open front door of the house and is gone.

The old lady stomps towards me, thumping the ground with her stick. She is looking directly at the camera. Her skin is criss-crossed with ancient wrinkles, spotted with big brownish freckles. Her hair sticks out from under her hat like cobwebs. The only smooth part of her is the apple of her cheeks. And then she says, "Did you get a picture?"

I shake my head, but she puts a finger to her lips and beckons me into the front garden. Slowly she lifts her stick and jabs it towards a tree. It takes a little while for me to see that she isn't pointing at a deer though.

Through the ferns and branches of overgrown shrubs I see a red squirrel. The sun is behind its blond ears. It's frozen, clinging upside down on a branch, its eyes shiny and black and surprised, its tail in a question mark. I hope the camera is pointing in the right direction because I don't dare let my eyes leave the moment with the rusty squirrel. I move a step forward, but the squirrel whips away and disappears into the tree.

"Did you get a picture that time?" the old lady says.

I nod, "Yes. But it's a film, not a photograph. I'll show my sister Jodie," I say. "She's doing the Furze Island Project."

"Whatever are they interfering with now?" she huffs.

"Do you see them all the time?" I ask. "The red squirrels, I mean. Do you know that they're rare? That's what Jodie and Adam told me. Adam is my sister's boyfriend, well, not exactly, but she likes him. They've been looking out for seabirds today and they'll want to know about the red squirrel. But I'm looking for deer."

She looks directly at me. I wonder if all old

people have knowing eyes like that. I wonder if Grandma had.

"Will that deer come back?"

"She will," the old lady says. "But I doubt she'll come back today. Deer are shy, they prefer to hide away from people."

"Did she swim over from the mainland?"

She looks startled for a moment. "No, this one has always lived here."

"She's not shy with you."

"No, because..." She's still watching me. She has a frown buried deeply around her eyes. It looks like it's been there a long time. "What is the film for?"

I don't know why I think it's all right to tell her. She lives on this island. It feels like I can say it easier here because it's separate from home and people I know. She doesn't know Grandad,

144

so she won't be disappointed or uncomfortable or compare him with how he used to be. She'll only know him from what I tell her now.

"My grandad's got Alzheimer's and he's forgetting everything and now he's forgotten me. I'm looking for things to film for him, to help him remember. My mum told me he used to go and see the deer with my grandma. He came here too."

"Dusk and dawn, East Beach," she says. "That's where the deer go."

I start to say nobody is allowed on the island at those times of the day, but she interrupts and says, "Yes, I know you won't be able to see them there."

I smile. "Can I come back here another day?"

"Yes," she says, "but quietly next time."

20.

I ASK LINUS TO COME WITH ME OUT ON GRANDAD'S boat that evening. We have our life jackets and Dad says it will have to be a short trip because, although the long summer night is light, Dad didn't get home from work very early.

"Stay in sight," Dad calls from Gorbreen slipway.

I've never been out in Grandad's boat with

anyone else but Grandad. It's a new experience. I teach Linus how to row, but we spend half the time turning in circles and bumping into banks. It makes the video camera judder each time we do.

"What exactly are you looking for?" Linus says. His hair is extra curly today and he has to keep pushing it back from his forehead. He's sweaty and I know it's hard rowing, but only if you're not used to it.

I don't want to say that I'm looking for Grandad and Grandma because that sounds ridiculous. But it is what I'm looking for. I try to make the words say what I mean without sounding daft.

"I'm not really sure yet. I keep thinking that I'm going to find something, but I don't know exactly what it is. I'm kind of looking for a bright memory of Grandad's."

Linus screws up his nose. "Memories aren't outside."

I try another way. "These are the facts I've got so far. Grandad and Grandma knew each other when they were children. Grandad had a boat all his life and Mum told me Grandma had a soft spot for deer. So they might have come out here in a boat and seen some deer. Last year when I was out in the boat with Grandad we saw a deer and he talked like it was kind of familiar. So I'm trying to recreate his memory in a film. And then hopefully he will remember something important he wanted to tell me."

Linus shrugs.

It sounds logical and simple. But why would that be a special journey that Grandad wanted to take me on? We've rowed out here a thousand times. Why didn't he tell anyone about it before?

And it doesn't seem to have anything to do with a whale. I don't know how to make all the pieces fit together. Not yet.

"Just keep your eyes open for deer," I say.

"Like your grandad and grandma did," Linus says, as if he's trying to convince himself of what I'm doing.

There's rustling as we bump into another bank and we see the dark stripe of tails ticking against white rumps as deer scatter into the long grass.

Linus laughs. "Like us," he whispers because I have my finger over my lips. A curlew sings and my mouth can't help smiling. For a moment I think he might be right. I wonder if one evening in Grandma and Grandad's past might be exactly the same as the one we're having now.

21.

THE GATE TO THE OLD LADY'S HOUSE IS AJAR, but she isn't in the front garden. Her front door is open and I go inside. I can't call out because if the deer is here I don't want to scare her away. My video camera is on.

There's a closed door on one side of me, an open one on the other. The kitchen is grey, camouflaged with dust and dirt. There are rows of tins with beetles and frilly woodlice clambering over them; thick webs spotted with flies curve in the corners. All the colour is in the white bread on the sink, orange peanuts on the windowsills, handfuls of fresh grass and wild flowers on a chair.

The hallway opens up. I see unopened letters yellowing on a table, addressed to Miss E Bennett.

Straight ahead another door is ajar into a brighter room.

Miss Bennett is in her splintered straw hat, hunched in a wicker chair outside the French windows, but as I creep in I'm distracted by a wall of framed photographs. I look closer. They're like a crowd of people standing shoulder to shoulder and on top of each other and beside each other, blurred in a fuzz of dust. The photographs are shades of brown or grey and all the people look out from behind the glass, like an audience.

I think about Grandad as if he's a photograph and he can't speak to tell me what it's like in there, inside the frame and behind the glass.

"Hello," I whisper, "hello, hello, hello," to all of the people in the pictures because I'm thinking that they're like Grandad and I don't mind too much that they can't answer me.

"My name is Hannah," I say to them. "I'm named after my grandma who died before I was born.

"You look nice," I say to the old-fashioned black and white picture of a girl a bit older than Jodie, who is in a rowing boat out at sea with Furze Island in the background. The girl is sheltering her eyes from the sun and her hand holds back her wavy hair. She is smiling and I wonder if it counts, that the smile she gave then could also be for whoever looks at her now. A camera is hanging from a strap around her neck.

"That's what I'm doing," I whisper to the girl in the picture. "Sort of anyway."

I'm not sure if they had video cameras back then. I zoom into her face; I wonder about the photographs she's taken, why she took them and if she was on a journey like me.

"What did you want to take photos of?" I whisper.

"Things not to be forgotten," Miss Bennett says.

I hadn't noticed she'd come in. She is as grey as the girl in the old photograph, still squinting now; she has the same roundish face only now it is scored with wrinkles.

"That's you, isn't it?" I say. "How old were you back then?"

It takes her a moment to say, "Nineteen

forty-two... so I would have been seventeen."

"What don't you want to forget?" It feels like a really important question because that's what I'm doing. Trying to make sure something isn't forgotten.

She turns away before she finishes speaking. "The person who took that photograph."

I hadn't expected that.

Miss Bennett puts a finger to her lips. She is eighty-eight years old and her hands are like fossils. She leads me outside. The deer is in her back garden.

"That's Fern," Miss Bennett says softly. "She comes most days, just like her mother did and her grandmother and great-grandmother before her."

My eyes are wide. She's known the deer for a long, long time! I think I've found another path to Grandad. She might know something about what happened to them in the war which might help me find out what Grandma and Grandad have to do with the deer. I have a million questions, but I know to be quiet for now.

Fern has ears like a mouse, black eyes and white spots on her golden sides and she holds her head up and looks at me as if to say, *I'm not sure about you.*

There are two wicker chairs on the patio. I walk very slowly and put the video camera on the small cane table between the chairs and check Fern is in the picture.

"Do you know what happened to the deer in the war?"

Miss Bennett shakes her head. Ancient sadness is in her eyes. "There was one terrible, terrible night," she murmurs.

She thumps across the garden with her walking stick. Fern watches her, but doesn't run away. I realise she's used to the sounds Miss Bennett makes, but not mine.

Miss Bennett looks out over the cliff top through the break in the wall. I follow her quietly and stand beside her and see where her eyes are looking, through the harbour entrance and away to the horizon. She pokes with her stick at the tumble of bricks around her feet. Fern is beside her now and Miss Bennett is talking as if to the deer. "The war took many things, didn't it?"

I think of all those photographs she has, her family from the past. I wonder how many of them didn't come back from the war. I wonder about the deer. Did something happen to them in the war? Something Grandad knows about too?

I wish I hadn't made Miss Bennett remember something that makes her so unhappy. The war was such a long time ago, but I think her memories are so strong that she still feels the sadness now.

"Sorry," I say.

"For what?" she says.

I daren't say anything else.

She breathes deeply and I copy her. I smell

the briny sea in the air. I feel how the outside rushes inside my chest and blows away everything uncomfortable. I taste it in my mouth. I hope Miss Bennett's bad memory will be carried out to sea with her breath.

"I don't think my grandad had a bad memory of the deer," I say. "He doesn't think like that. I don't think he would have wanted me to know about something sad. He always sees the good in things."

Her hand loosens around the handle of her stick. She strokes Fern. "Only one good thing did survive from the island that night."

The atmosphere between us feels wrong, and I don't want Miss Bennett to still hurt, so I try to change the subject.

"Do you think the sea might be the greatest power on earth?" I ask.

"No," she says. "War was."

And I think she's still thinking of something terrible that happened then.

22.

OTHER LOST GRANDADS AND GRANDMAS ARE IN the television room at East Harbour Care Home, their necks drooping; their distant eyes scare me a bit. And then I think that there must be lots of other grandchildren like Linus and me.

Mark, a physiotherapist who is helping Grandad with his movement, meets us out in the hallway.

"How is he?" Mum asks.

"Fine," Mark smiles. He's saying what I always used to say and I guess that means he's trying to protect us, or trying to hide something. He nods towards the video camera and speaks to me. "As far as his memory and mood go, the more you can do to help him, the better. It's a bit like he's stranded in a small place, but we can help by reaching out to him."

"Like on an island?" I say.

"That's it," Mark says, surprised. "Just like that."

All the cheerfulness and gentleness are still missing from Grandad's face. Now he looks like everyone else in the TV room, like anybody's grandad. I hate that I even think that.

It takes a little while of everyone chatting and telling Grandad lots of times that it's us before the ocean of nothing clears a little from his eyes.

He reaches for my hand. It looks like the same hand it has always been. But how can such a big strong hand feel so papery and fragile?

"I've got something to show you," I say.

He babbles something. It sounds like he's having a conversation with someone from when he worked in the boatyard, but none of us are quite sure what it's about. Jodie and I look each other in the eye, to make each other braver.

Jodie puts her laptop on Grandad's lap and we link it to the video camera. Jodie helped me edit the film so that all the boring bits (like Josh and the sausage and beans) got cut out, and all the good bits (like the harbour and the deer) follow each other like a story. I talk to Grandad while we watch and describe what is happening in my film: our house, Linus and his scooter on Southbrook Hill, Mum talking and the trip on the ferry to the island. Grandad's lips tremble and I think he tries to smile and every now and then his eyes brighten.

"I think he's seeing things he remembers," I say.

Somewhere, shining through his slumped body and drooping mouth, we can all see a little bit of Grandad as he used to be. And it only takes a tiny bit of remembering him like he was to make us all feel good.

"Hannah, I think you've found your talent here," Dad says, while we watch the film.

"She has, hasn't she?" Mum smiles widely. "This is a beautiful film for all of us. What a great thing to keep for our future too."

"Even Grandad's smiling," Jodie says.

"Imagine if someone was grumpy and miserable their whole life," Mum says, "how little the family would be left with."

"Like Miss Bennett," I say.

"Who's Miss Bennett?" Dad says.

"She's a very old lady who lives on Furze Island. I think she's been unhappy most of her life. Except when she was a girl because she looked happy in a photograph when she was seventeen."

Mum and Dad look at each other, a question in their eyebrows.

"How do you know her?" Dad says.

"I visited her," I say and then realise what that means.

"Jodie?" Mum asks and Jodie is gritting her teeth.

"I didn't know! I can't look after Hannah the whole time," Jodie says. "I've got important things to do."

"With that boy Adam?" Mum says.

"Who's Adam?" Dad snaps.

And then there's a whole discussion, which

is nearly a row, about Jodie's responsibilities and me not going off on my own into a house with someone they don't know. It's only then, with the film still running and nobody talking to Grandad, that I suddenly see the change and hear the soft groan that comes from him. And we all look because none of the other things matter except that Grandad might be trying to remember us.

His smile is gathering; he laughs. And then he says it. It isn't clear, but I'm sure I hear right. "The whale," he says, as if there's something in front of him now. "It was a whale." He reaches his arms out as if he is trying to hold on to something.

I press pause on the camera and there on the film is what I recorded at Miss Bennett's house. Fern the deer. But how can Fern remind him of a whale? Is it something else earlier in the film? Is it just luck that at this moment he happens to remember the whale? But Grandad babbles and mutters and we can't work out what he's saying. He draws his arms into himself, as if he's holding someone small in his arms, but there's nothing there. "There, there," he says. "Safe now."

On the way home nobody feels like I do, that Grandad is still trying to tell me about a whale. They all keep saying that maybe Grandad is getting confused and that he's remembering saying it before he had the stroke, because there's nothing on the film to do with a whale. That's not what I think at all. I think the whale is becoming more important than ever. But Dad is mostly stressed about me going to Miss Bennett's.

"We don't know her," he says.

"But she's really old and sad and lonely," I say,

trying to make him sympathise.

"That's as may be, but it's not your responsibility to look after the old people of this world," Dad says. "I want you to stay with Jodie from now on."

Jodie rolls her eyes.

"But Grandad saw something on the film and it might have been at Miss Bennett's house," I say. "It might be the one important thing that he wanted to tell me." And I want to know more than ever.

"Hannah, we all want Grandad to get better. There are other things you can film. We'd all like to hang on to what we think will help his memory, but we have to face the fact that Alzheimer's makes him say and do things he wouldn't normally."

Mum sighs. "His mobility is improving. We all need a little hope."

"There's hope and there's reality," Dad mutters.

Grandad's memories are real. I'm sure of it. There are more paths now, more things that are leading me somewhere. Closer to the whale?

23.

Miss Bennett has sad memories of the war. I think about that a lot. If I keep asking her about the war and the deer, I'm going to make her unhappy. I need to find something good for her to talk about. I need to find something good and make it bigger, because I'm hoping to find another path to Grandad.

Jodie's not going to Furze Island today, but I

ask her to take me down to the museum at the quay, to see if there's anything there about the war. She doesn't agree straight away, but makes a phone call with her bedroom door shut and then comes out and says, "Fine." I'm not sure why she's so moody.

We call for Linus on the way. I've got my video camera and binoculars that I take everywhere with me now.

"Remember you said you saw a whale on the TV?" I ask, running to keep up with Linus on his scooter. "Did you see the one that's in the English Channel?"

"Slow down," Jodie says, catching us up. "It's not a race."

"Yeah, it was on the news," Linus says, "but they haven't said any more about it. I expect it's gone now."

"Do you remember where exactly it was though?"

"Near Dover I think, you know, where the ferry goes to France. I think people on the ferry saw it."

"Maybe Grandad went on that ferry once."

Jodie rolls her eyes, "Not that again. It's two hundred miles away at least. It won't still be there."

"I know that," I say.

"I think you're on a wild goose chase," she mutters. "You know as well as I do that people with Alzheimer's put things in the wrong place and forget things. And they say things that don't mean anything. They get their words wrong."

I hold Jodie's arm, but she looks impatient to keep going. I stop her. Linus scoots on, freewheeling down the rest of Southbrook Hill.

"I'm looking for the greatest power on earth

and all you are is moody. Why do you have to make things sound so hopeless?"

She sighs and I know she's trying hard not to be mean. "I don't want you to do all this and then find out there's nothing at the end." Her face softens. "I don't want you to get hurt."

"I won't," I say. Because I truly believe that nothing to do with Grandad will ever hurt me.

Jodie's girlfriend meets her outside the museum and they go and sit on the wall by the quay and I leave the binoculars and camera with them because you're not allowed to film in there. Linus leaves his scooter with them too and we go inside.

We go straight to the room with things from the war. In the display cabinets are toys made of tin, tins of food, kitchen things that are exactly the same as at Miss Bennett's house, bullet shells, ration books and gas masks, bronze and beige, khaki and green. There's a memorial wall with postcards and letters and photographs of soldiers.

"Over here," Linus says, "there's stuff about Furze Island."

There's a little room to the side. There are photographs of the harbour and island during the war, typewritten captions underneath them. There's a photo of a sailing boat filled with refugees from Holland, mothers and clinging babies, dirty children, shivering grandmothers, fishermen and their boys, their possessions wrapped in scarves.

Another photo is of trenches of daffodils and a herd of deer hiding among them. Another of Furze Island shattered and black, trees stunted and broken, the beaches guarded by rolls of barbed wire. There's another of some cottages left in the charred remains; one of them I recognise as Miss Bennett's house. But that's not what's making my heart race. It's the name of the photographer. Eva Bennett.

24.

"Is she Sleeping Beauty or something," Jodie says, trying to see through the gap in the gate at Miss Bennett's house, "because she can't have had any visitors for at least a hundred years."

"It might be because they can't get in," I say.

I know I'm not supposed to be at Miss Bennett's house, but Jodie is on my side and I convince her that nothing can go wrong, that it's more important for me to find out about the deer and, who knows, it might even lead me to Grandad's whale. And I'm sure Miss Bennett can help *me* if I find a way to help *her* remember, without making her sad. Jodie's changed her mood, but I think she's playing along with me, being ultra-cheerful, saying maybe there is something here that would remind Grandad. I think it's because Adam is with her though.

I ask Jodie and Adam if they'll chop back the overgrown bushes around Miss Bennett's gate.

"Are you sure she wants us to cut this much?" Jodie says, passing branches to Adam.

"Not exactly," I say.

"Hannah!" Jodie splutters.

"You'd want it cut down if it got like this, wouldn't you?" Which I think is a good argument. I'm about to go through Miss Bennett's gate.

"I won't say anything if you don't."

Jodie closes her eyes and puts her fingers in her ears because that way she can pretend, if Dad asks, that she didn't know I went to Miss Bennett's again.

I walk through the house. Miss Bennett is in her back garden. The tall brick wall curves at the bottom of her garden, only a few steps away from the edge of the cliff. She stumbles on some of the broken bricks to look out of the gap in the wall.

"What made the wall fall down?" I ask her.

She knocks at a loose brick with her stick and it falls away and opens the view even more.

"Old age," Miss Bennett says. "Everything old falls down."

I collect up the bricks and stack them in a pile and clear away all the fallen rubble so that she can get closer to the cliff edge without tripping over.

I carry the wicker chairs over so we can sit by the gap in the wall and I watch the sea through Grandad's binoculars.

"Have you always lived on Furze Island?" I ask.

"This has been my family home for quite a few generations."

"Have you ever seen a whale in the harbour?"

She hesitates. "No," she says. "A whale wouldn't be able to get in here. I would know if one had. "

"That's what Adam said."

Is there any point in watching the harbour? I'm curious about the red boats though. They're back, the divers bobbing like seals in the water. A thick rope net is being lowered by the crane.

"Have you heard what they've found down there?" I say, pointing. "It's a wreck of something. They said on the news that they think it might be an old boat." I hand Miss Bennett the binoculars.

I thought she'd like to see what's happening, but Miss Bennett looks through the binoculars as if she isn't interested and leaves them in her lap as I pick up my video camera and switch it on. I focus on the big boat alongside the red ones, and the men waving their arms as the crane lowers the net into the water.

"Grandad and I used to go out in his boat all the time, but we can't now because he's in a care home. He had his boat from when he was a boy."

Miss Bennett says, "Most boats were commandeered during the war or camouflaged so they couldn't be seen during an air raid. My father kept his boat hidden in our boathouse further down the cliff."

I notice she can't help talking about the war. I think about how long ago it was, how she still keeps it alive in her memory.

"You must remember lots of things from back then, especially if you took photographs. I saw some in the museum."

She tilts her head up a little; the creases are deep in her face.

"You and I have something in common then," she says. She looks out to sea. "Like you, I took pictures to hold on to the past. War made the future… unreliable." She shakes her head and stops talking.

She doesn't realise that just hearing Grandad talk every day about things I don't know matters to me. Grandad didn't really talk of the war because he was just a boy then, but I remember he once told me that he'd heard the deathly drone of German bombers in the sky.

"Weren't you afraid?" I'd asked him.

"I should have been," he'd said. "I didn't want

to be in the underground shelter, imagining. I had no idea what the war meant, what sacrifice and love were, until I went outside and saw for myself what I felt thundering right through me. Our hearts are tender when we're young; we only want to fill them. And fill them we did."

I just want to hear anything that makes me feel like I did when I was with him, kind of excited and peaceful at the same time. He shared all sorts of things about his life with me, just as I did with him every day after school. But not everything.

"Please tell me more. I do want to know," I say to Miss Bennett. "I don't mind if it's about the war." I look through the binoculars again, giving her time to decide. The men in the red boats are leaning over the side, waiting for something to happen. "Maybe what those divers have found in the harbour is something from the war."

The wicker chair creaks as Miss Bennett leans forward. Sawdust puffs from tiny dark woodworm holes peppered in the legs of the chair as she cracks her stick on the ground and talks of bullets and bombs. The chair is crumbling and turning to dust like everything in her kitchen.

"Alzheimer's is like the war," I say.

"Things you can't see can have a big effect," she says softly.

"Like a disease that you can only see under a microscope," I say. "And small things do too. Like the tiny tablets people take to make them better. Only there's nothing like that we can give Grandad."

Miss Bennett's soft powdery cheeks relax.

"When I showed Grandad my film, he seemed to remember something when he saw the recording of your house and Fern," I say. "But he said we were going to find a whale."

Miss Bennett looks surprised and then suddenly we both laugh, because we're both picturing a whale. And it's the biggest creature in the world and all the small things just seem tiny and insignificant, just for a moment.

"What's your grandad's name?"

"Arthur Jenkins," I say. "He lived around Hambourne all his life, but he's younger than you. Did you know him?"

She thinks for a minute, and I think she might be hoping she can help me. She hesitates, taking a long time to say, "No... no, I don't think so. Apart from a few years during the war, I've always lived here."

Then she says, "Wait here," and goes back inside for a minute. I watch the divers through the video camera. The ropes strain as the crane hoists something from the seabed.

Miss Bennett returns. She says it's not what she was looking for, but shows me an old photograph of Furze Island taken from the quay. The morning sun is low and the shadows are long. The island is complete, with trees, the quay and the stone cottages, and written along the bottom is the date, May 24th 1942.

Miss Bennett squints at me. Is she trying to work out something?

"Refugees from Holland were given temporary sanctuary on the island, but we were all evacuated to the mainland that day. War took away our shared memories, and those of the refugees who'd lost their homes and families. I wanted something we could keep, before it was all destroyed."

I think of Grandad then, as if he's a refugee,

lost in a world where he hardly knows who we were or where he was. But I see Miss Bennett is feeling easier now. She sits down and continues.

"Not long after that, a film crew came down from London and spent some time rigging Furze Island with explosives. They made a decoy, to fool German bombers into thinking the island was the main harbour. Navigation systems weren't entirely accurate in those days, so the explosions and fires were supposed to draw the bombs away to protect the harbour and the people who lived there. But the wildlife wasn't accounted for."

She sighs and her breath is like the tide. "The island was on fire and the deer swam away."

She looks tired with sadness, shrunken by a terrible memory, but my eyes keep switching to the harbour. Yellow balloons pop up from under the water, alongside the lifting crane. The water parts as a long black back breaks the surface.

"I'm sorry, Miss Bennett," I gasp, "but I have to go! I need to see Grandad."

25.

"It's not regular visiting hours, he's just had his lunch," the receptionist at East Harbour Care Home says. "Did you come on your own?"

I caught the ferry and a bus on my own, but right now it really doesn't seem important. I know I'll be in trouble with everyone when I get home, but they'll understand when I tell them that I've found the journey Grandad wanted to take me on.

I imagine how happy they'll be that I've found the whale that Grandad remembered. Only it isn't a whale!

"My parents are busy working and my sister is busy and Miss Bennett was talking about the war today and how a decoy fooled German bombers." I'm talking too much when I just want her to let me see Grandad. "It's really important. I saw something in the harbour and Grandad said we were going to find a whale, but I think he said the wrong word."

"Is that so?" the receptionist says.

"Yes, but that's because he's got Alzheimer's! I couldn't wait for my parents to finish work and bring me. Normally Grandad and I spend the summer holidays together, except he's here instead."

The receptionist's eyebrows rise further and

further up her forehead as she listens. But she's not moving quickly enough for me.

"If I don't tell him today then it might be too late," I say. "I need to find something out before the eighteenth of August."

"I see," she says. "Sounds urgent."

"Exactly," I say, leaning across the reception counter. "Some people in my family don't seem to have much hope for Grandad's memory, but I do."

She smiles. I have to sit and wait for lunch to be cleared she tells me, but I can't sit still. I go back and stand by the reception until the lady looks up at me.

"Have you got any books here?" I ask. "Because I want to show Grandad a picture from the war."

Eventually she takes me to a bookcase in the television room and I find what I'm looking for. Then the receptionist leads me to Grandad's room and tells me I have just fifteen minutes before she'll be back to collect me.

Grandad is sitting in a chair by the window; the net curtain rolls and I see him enjoying the softness of the breeze on his face.

I hesitate. It isn't like all those times I've come home from school, eager to talk to him, eager to hear him. But I hate thinking of him in any other way. I just have to imagine it is still him in there, somewhere.

"Grandad, it's me, Hannah. Did they do your toast nice this morning?" I say. "I miss you being at home and so do the birds, and Smokey isn't scared of me like he is of you. He's taking more of them, I know he is, but I don't know how to stop him."

I kneel by Grandad's feet and hold both his hands. I know he feels my touch. For just a moment his eyes catch mine.

"Grandad, it's Hannah. I miss you."

And then I tell him about the divers and the wreck they've found and play him my film on the small video camera screen. We watch the red boats and the crane hoist and we hear Miss Bennett talk of the war.

"Something was sunk and now they've brought it up to the surface. I think it might be one of these."

More than anything I want to believe Grandad will remember.

For a moment I'd thought that the sandbank in the harbour was a whale. I think of those German bombers being fooled by what they saw. Nobody knew anything about a whale. Grandad had never travelled and it was impossible for one to come into the harbour. So I guess that Grandad might have made a mistake too.

I open the book to a picture spread across two pages, a grainy black and white drawing. I put it on his lap and point.

"Look, Grandad."

Grandad's eyes slowly find the picture. A smile quivers in the corner of his mouth, but his eyes roam away.

"Grandad, see this book?" His eyes turn down again. "It's a picture from the war. Do you remember when you were a boy and saw a submarine?"

His lips tremble, but I know he isn't really looking.

"Hannah," he smiles, "is it time for breakfast?" But I don't know whether he means Grandma Hannah or me.

"You've had breakfast and lunch, Grandad. Please look at the book."

Instead he stares towards the window. I hold up the book, put it in front of him so he has to look.

"Grandad, what happened with the submarine? Was it a submarine you wanted us to find again? Grandad, was the journey to do with the deer and the war and a submarine?"

You can't tell any more who Grandad used to be. He could have been a bank robber or a prime minister, an elephant farmer or a brain surgeon. He was a boy during the war and then a boatbuilder and then my grandad. But he doesn't recognise me and I hardly recognise him.

"I think it was a submarine you wanted to tell me about, Grandad, not a whale."

No matter how many times I say it, he doesn't remember.

"Is war the greatest power on earth? Is it the sea?"

I see in his eyes that he knows I'm expecting an answer. But we both know he can't find one to give me.

Mum and Dad are late home so Jodie covers for me. Luckily one of her friends saw me get on the ferry, but she tells me never to come back on my own again; she doesn't care how important I think it is because she's the one who'll be in trouble. I don't tell her what happened, I just say that I needed to see Grandad and that makes her stop going on at me.

Smokey sits on the fence and lords himself over *our* territory, high up and safely away from the hosepipe. I feed the sparrows and watch while they busy themselves, but there's a lot less of them than before. I throw a handful of seeds at Smokey and he hisses and springs away.

26.

THE SUN HAS BAKED THE GROUND HARD AND the air is warm and lazy and smells of coconut. Holiday aeroplanes hum high in the sky, but it all makes me feel heavy and as though I'm somewhere unfamiliar.

Fern is in the grey kitchen eating the leaves and grass that Miss Bennett has left on her table. I move slowly and she lets me come quite close before she walks away from me, through the house, and I follow her to where Miss Bennett is in the cool of the sitting room. She has taken all her photographs down and is dusting them.

"You left in a hurry yesterday," she says.

"I'm sorry. I went to see my grandad. I told him about the submarine they found in the harbour. I really thought it might help him remember something from the past."

"Did he?"

I shake my head.

Miss Bennett's eyes have turned down and I wonder if she feels sorry that I don't have better news.

"Do you remember a submarine from the war, in the harbour?"

She shakes her head. But she doesn't seem to be listening and I wonder if she's thinking about

Grandad instead. I don't want anyone else telling me that there's no hope for him.

Fern sniffs at a bunch of flowers in a china vase. She starts to eat them. I don't think Miss Bennett minds; in fact, I think she probably left them there for her. I walk closer and hold out my hand, but Fern is still nervous of me.

The photograph that Miss Bennett showed me yesterday is on the table.

"Miss Bennett?" I say. I lean against the big table and watch her wipe a frame and hang it back on the wall. Fern stands beside Miss Bennett. I do care that Miss Bennett has sad memories, but I need to find another path back to Grandad. There is no whale so I need to ask her more about the deer and the war. I'm running out of time. I have to find out what's so important to Grandad about August 18th.

"Miss Bennett, you know you told me before that one thing survived that terrible night during that war? What was it?"

Miss Bennett gently touches the white spots on Fern's back. The soft dapples remind me of sun and shadows on the ground in the harbour banks. I want to be able to touch her too, but I know Miss Bennett and Fern are special together.

"Sorry, I didn't mean to leave in the middle of what you were telling me yesterday," I say. "Please."

Miss Bennett opens the drawer at the end of the table and rummages through lots of photographs. She picks out two. The first is similar to the one in the museum, a field full of daffodils and a herd of deer.

"The daffodil fields on Furze Island were full of flowers once the island recovered after the war.

We grew them here, sold them at Covent Garden in London. Thousands upon thousands of golden crowns flourished." Miss Bennett watches Fern as she speaks. "And then one spring after the war I saw the daffodil heads were missing. Some deer must have survived on the mainland and then swum out to Furze. They were eating all the flowers!"

She shows me the other photograph of her as a young woman in the garden here. She has a deer with her.

"There was only one deer from the island that survived that night during the war. I called her Fern. I looked after her on the mainland with me until I could move back here."

"It wasn't this Fern though, was it?" I didn't think deer could live *that* long.

"No. Fern is only two years old. It was another deer, her great-great-great, I forget how many greats, but her grandmother. I called the whole family of them Fern. She was the only one on the island for a while until the others swam over."

"Why did you call all the deer Fern?" I say.

She shakes her duster and clumps of dust fall on the carpet. She wipes some more frames.

"Is it because you couldn't think of anything else?" I ask.

"No," she says. She picks up the next picture, one of an older lady, who looks a little like Miss Bennett.

"Was it because of someone you knew called Fern?" I guess. I feel the tension in the still air. "Because of someone, like your grandmother?"

She gently wipes the dust away with her hand.

"Some things you want to go on forever, even if all you have is a name." She leans heavily on her stick. "But sometimes it's better to forget." She says it sharply and I realise I've asked too much. I've made her look into the past and see something she didn't want to see.

I feel like I'm sinking now too. What if

Grandad's memory is a bad one too? What if something terrible had happened with a submarine? What if Miss Bennett is right and it's better to forget? Then I think of Grandad's memory. Had I asked too many questions? Had I worn his memory out?

"Sorry," I say. I hang my head.

"For what this time?"

"Asking too many questions."

She shakes her head and looks at me with gentle eyes. She seems to know what I'm thinking because she says, "It's the disease. There's nothing you did to your grandad that could have caused it. We all want to hold on to the good things from our past and leave the rest behind. But it's not been easy for me."

She hands me the framed photograph. I climb on the table and hang it up for her, matching the paler shape left on the wall where it had been before.

I climb down and she carries on dusting. I look in the drawer at the end of the table. There's a chunky black and silver camera with a leather strap.

"Miss Bennett? Will you come round the island with me and teach me to take good pictures?"

But it's all been too much. "No," she says. "Leave me be now."

I didn't know how much that would sting.

I pass Jodie and Adam who are still clearing gorse along paths nearby.

"What's wrong? Where are you going?" Jodie calls.

"I don't know."

I go down the steps and along South Beach

where Grandad had walked me out into the sea. It's all my fault. I suddenly hate that everything's about the past. What about the future?

27.

I ASK IF WE CAN GO AND VISIT GRANDAD AGAIN.

He is sitting in the television room with the other lost grandads and grandmas.

I wrap Grandad's hand in both of mine and I still can't hold it all, but there's nothing else to hold on to. Touching him seems to wake him for a moment.

"Tell me about the submarine, Grandad," I say.

"Did you see a submarine in the harbour in the war? Do you remember a fire on Furze Island? Did you know Grandma then? Do you remember what happened to the deer? Did you know Fern?"

The ocean of nothing fills his eyes.

"Hannah," Mum says, "too many questions. You're confusing him."

I know I shouldn't do that, but I'm desperate for something more from him. I can't think bigger without him.

"Grandad, it was a submarine, wasn't it?" I say.

"What's that you're asking him?" Dad says.

"She's talking about the wreck *we* saw in the harbour," Jodie says, nodding towards the television. "Look, it's on the news."

I know the look Jodie gives me then is to make sure Dad thinks we were together when we saw it being lifted. I can't tell them what happened with Miss Bennett.

There's footage on the TV of the discovery in the harbour. A small Second World War submarine with a huge hole blasted in its side has been rusting away in the deeper channel and they are talking of restoring it and putting it in the museum.

I point at the television. "Look, Grandad. The submarine I was telling you about. Do you remember the submarine? Where were we going on a journey, Grandad? Was it to do with the war? Was it in the harbour?"

"When did you tell him about a submarine?" Dad asks.

But I see Mum shake her head at him. She takes me in her arms and holds me tight.

"It's all right," she whispers into my hair. "I miss him too. We want to remember him as he

207

used to be, but we have to try and see him as he is now so we know how to… how to be with him the best we can."

"Why can't we take him home now?" I say. "He doesn't want to be here, he wants to be home with us. I can help look after him. He'll get much better if we're with him all the time."

I know the Alzheimer's won't get any better, but the people in the care home said his speech and mobility are improving a little. And now and again there were moments when he was vivid and just as he'd always been.

"We should tell her," Dad says to Mum. "It's only fair."

"Dad, he won't be too much trouble; he'd want to be with us," I say.

Mum closes her eyes.

"Listen, Hannah," Dad says, "it wasn't our

idea to put Grandad in a home." I see him take a breath. I can tell he's trying to steady himself and that makes me more scared of what he's about to tell me. "A while back, when Grandad was first diagnosed with Alzheimer's, he made us promise that if he was to do something that… worried us, we were to move him to a home. He didn't want to be a burden to us; he wanted us to be free to get on with our own lives."

I shrink as Dad says it.

I'm shocked that it was Grandad who'd made that decision, that he thought we wouldn't want to take care of him.

"But why? Doesn't he think we love him?"

"Of course he does," Mum says softly. "But I think he's always loved us even more."

And then I hear a voice from the local newsreader on the television say, "… *not far along the coast from the harbour where the submarine was found, there's been another unusual sighting today. The humpback whale has only been recorded off the south coast a handful of times since records began. Despite this rare and extraordinary sighting, it is also one of concern to marine welfare organisations as to why the whale would be so far off its usual course..."*

"Jodie!" I say. She's as wide-eyed as me.

Grandad's eyes rise to the television and I see a flicker in his eyebrows, as if he's searching through files, trying to catch a memory. He looks at me; his old smile gathers around his eyes.

I go round the back of Grandad's chair and lean my head on his shoulder, wrap my arms round his wide chest and lay my hands on his heart. His one hand folds round both of mine.

"I'm going to find the whale, Grandad." I whisper. "I'm going to find it for you."

28.

I TAKE THE BINOCULARS AND MY CAMERA TO FURZE Island the next day, to watch the horizon for the whale. If only I could film it and show Grandad. I don't know why, but I'm so convinced by Grandad's old smile, so sure now that it is a whale he wanted us to find after all, not a submarine. I'll try anything, but the best place to see beyond the harbour is from Miss Bennett's house up on the cliff top, on the east side of the island.

On the ferry over I tell Jodie what had happened with Miss Bennett.

"Don't go and see her today," she says.

I try and think of a good answer because I need her on my side.

"If I don't talk about the war then she's fine. So I'll just talk about nice things." I know that Miss Bennett lives apart from the rest of the world for her own reasons, but that she's happy to share her house with any animals that want to join her. And I choose to be with her too. "She's got the best view from her house," I say. "I might be able to see the whale from there."

"It's not here, Hannah, it's further along the coast."

"I don't care," I say. "They said it's closer to here now and I'm going to try to film it for Grandad."

And then Jodie says, "Is that her?"

Miss Bennett is at Furze Island quay. Her walking stick is hooked over the back of a wheelchair, her camera round her neck. She waves away the lady from the visitor centre who is pushing her.

Jodie puts her arm across my shoulders and walks up to Miss Bennett with me.

"You must be Jodie," Miss Bennett says. "Hannah has told me lots about you."

Jodie nods and bites her lip.

Miss Bennett closes her eyes and her face softens. "I'm not used to having inquisitive children around," she says, knowing we need some kind of explanation. "Was it you who cut the gorse by my back gate?"

Jodie twitches her mouth; she doesn't seem sure whether she should admit it. "Yes, me and Adam, but—"

"Thank you," Miss Bennett says.

My mouth wants to smile and I am trying hard not to. In fact, I just want to spring on Miss Bennett and tell her she's lovely and I am so glad she's here.

"Don't upset Hannah," Jodie says in her big-sister voice. "She's having a tough time at the moment. But I expect you know that."

Miss Bennett straightens her back and nods slowly to Jodie.

"All right?" Jodie says to me. "I'll be cutting back more gorse where I was before." She squeezes my arm. "You know where I am if you need me," and she runs to catch up with Adam who's gone on with the others.

"Well," Miss Bennett says, "what shall we take pictures of?"

29.

"WHEN WAS THE LAST TIME YOU WENT AROUND the island?"

"I don't remember. Maybe this year, maybe many years ago. All the days blur into one now. Some days I can't tell the past from the present."

"That's what a memory is," I say. "Something from the past we remember today."

"So it is," she says. "Quite a mystery really."

We spy a fidgety red squirrel and I squat beside Miss Bennett and film while she waits patiently with her camera. I film for six minutes while Miss Bennett takes only one photograph of the squirrel with the sun on its golden back. She explains that because you only have twenty-four chances with the film in the type of camera she has, you have to take your time and wait for the right moment. I think about that when I'm filming afterwards, taking more time to get in the right position, to see the best possible picture first.

I push Miss Bennett to the cliff edge near to her house, where you can almost see down to the edge of East Beach. She looks up from the camera at the view and back to her camera lens, moving a little to one side to change the angle and get the perfect picture.

"I've taken this picture many times before," she says.

"Grandad once told me that nothing stays the same because the world doesn't keep still for a minute," I say.

"True," Miss Bennett smiles. "But in comparison, memories feel as solid as rocks."

She frowns, at herself, like she's made a mistake. "Maybe they're not," she mumbles, I think because she suddenly remembers that Grandad has Alzheimer's.

I ask her to teach me to take good pictures. I learn loads in just a few minutes about how much sky and sea looks right, how something in the foreground reflects something in the distance, about how a picture can tell a whole story if the right elements are captured together. I realise then that all her photographs are the things she's keeping alive all by herself.

"I really wanted to go to your house, to watch the harbour entrance and look out to sea," I say. "A whale is out there and I'm hoping to film it."

"Yes, I heard about it," she says.

Miss Bennett unhooks her walking stick and gets out of the wheelchair.

"Follow me," she says. "There's an even better view."

You couldn't see the other path near to her house, not at first. It is thick with ferns and crowded with long grass. Under my feet I can feel the edge of a step. I go ahead and hold Miss Bennett's arm to steady her as we climb down. We come out on a kind of sandy ledge that slopes down to East Beach, where the shore is narrow, way past the Keep Out sign. Then she stops and knocks back some ferns.

Hidden behind the ferns is the boathouse I'd seen from the beach, its wooden doors faded grey, with thin windows at the top just under the roof.

"Is this yours?" I say.

"You'll see," she says. She has a key in her pocket and undoes the rusty lock. "This boathouse is one of the few things here that survived the war."

Inside it smells of dust and old varnish; I remember the smell from somewhere. From around the quay? Maybe Grandad?

A wooden rowing boat, about as long as a car, rests on a trailer with wheels. It's the same boat from the picture of Miss Bennett when she was seventeen.

She smoothes the bow and I see the curve roll under her hand.

Miss Bennett smiles. "I was always out in the boat as a child, taking photographs. My father gave the boat to me, when he went off to war," she says. "But I haven't been out in her for many years.

"You're younger and a lot smaller, but the memory plays tricks." She looks at me. "I knocked down the wall," she says quietly. "I knocked it down and there you were in the sea with your camera. For a moment I thought I was looking into the past, at myself."

I think that's why she let me in. Because I'm like her.

You can see right out through the harbour from here. I look out to the wide sky and the sea vanishing far, far away past the land. I've only heard about the whale. But, even zooming in with my video camera to the wide horizon, I know the whale will seem tiny and be very hard to find.

"That's where the poor deer swam, out there," Miss Bennett says. "They were confused because of the smoke blowing onshore. They swam the wrong way."

I see where the sea disappears, curving over the earth. I realise there is no land out there, nowhere to go. Miss Bennett stares at something far away in the past. It wasn't the bombs or fire that killed the deer. They were too scared to stay here. I think of those deer swimming and swimming and swimming, looking for somewhere safe to go. My heart aches, just as hers must have done, knowing that they'd gone for good.

I've reminded her once again of the terrible memory. But there must be something good I can find for her, something she can hold on to.

30.

"Can I look inside?" I ask.

She takes off her hat and pushes her cobweb hair away from her face. "Why not," she says.

I climb on the trailer and go round the edge, unhooking the tarpaulin cover and rolling it back to the stern. Underneath are three bench seats and the oars. I sit on the middle seat and a smile lights Miss Bennett's face. It's the boat that she loves.

"Shall we go out in it?"

"I'm a decrepit old lady. I won't be going out in any boat."

"Just pretend," I say, feeding the oars into their sockets. "I'll row and you can sit at the stern, and I'll pretend to take you away from the island."

I laugh, imagining it, at me hardly big enough to reach the oars properly and Miss Bennett in her crumpled hat watching the sea pass under us.

Miss Bennett's cheeks ruffle into a smile and before I can say anything more she's reaching her hand out for me to take her camera and saying, "Come on then, help me in!"

Right then Miss Bennett is as beautiful as the statue on the quay; we are just like those smooth bronze people with no names. I realise now what Mrs Gooch had been talking about. That there are moments in our life, just like a piece of art, that are golden. And whenever we see something similar we'll be reminded of them, all wrapped up in the smell of varnish and the smoothness of the wood, the taste of the sea and the sizzle of the waves below us. I'll remember, and Miss Bennett will remember, this day and our memory will be a good one.

With a lot of help, Miss Bennett climbs in slowly, one leg at a time. She huffs and coughs for a bit, but sits down at the stern facing me and thumps her stick on the bottom of the boat.

"Well, I haven't done that in a while," she says, still smiling and catching her breath. She holds up her camera and I get ready for her to take a picture.

"No need to smile," she said, which isn't what people usually say when they take a photograph.

"Pick up the oars, that's it, arms out in front of you. Look to the left, as if you're looking over the side of the boat."

She continues with instructions: lean back a bit, chin down, relax your elbows just a little and so on, until I am just how she wants me and then she is silent.

She only takes one picture of me. I want a copy; I want to see me as she does.

I give her my camera to film me.

"Where are we heading?" Miss Bennett chuckles.

I hesitate, but I think I know what I'm doing.

I pretend to row and tell her a new story. We are children and this is our boat, our new adventure. I tell her we hear the curlew singing, soft and eerie; we see a fawn lying safe, where its skin blends in as if it's part of the landscape. We have to whisper, but there's no need to worry because it's hidden in the dapple of shadows that shelter it. I watch as Miss Bennett believes in our dream, as we make a new memory. I watch the horizon over her shoulder for the whale, until the video camera clicks and runs out of power.

When I leave Miss Bennett, she smiles. It's the same ancient skin, but her smile looks new. I feel something is changing and I'm nervous.

"My cousin's great-niece has been writing to me for some time. She has a big house in Yorkshire with a wide view of the moors."

My heart sinks and Miss Bennett knows.

"It's been a long time since I could say that I enjoyed someone's company. I think it's about time I tried a little harder. Keep an eye on the deer for me," she says. "Just now and again."

I don't want her to go. Not now.

"Sorry," she says.

"What for?" I ask, my lips trembling.

"That I couldn't help you find the whale."

I shrug; it's all I can do.

She curves her hand round my cheek. "But I don't doubt you'll find it."

31.

WE ARE ON THE FERRY BOAT GOING BACK TO THE quay. I tell Jodie Miss Bennett is leaving.

"I know you miss having Grandad around," Jodie says, wrapping me against the wind, "but Miss Bennett's not like him."

Was that what I'd been trying to do? Find someone to replace Grandad? Never.

"She's just had a lot of horrible memories. I

think she lost a lot of her family in the war and she's been sad and alone ever since. You'd be the same if something horrible happened to Adam."

Jodie shrugs.

I sigh and try to blow away what aches inside.

I lean over the railings and rest my chin on my hands. My head is too heavy to hold up. I think of how, even though I love my family and lots of other people, Grandad is the one person I need the most. Maybe because he understands me more than anyone else. Maybe because when we're together we think bigger, and we are somehow… bigger.

I watch the rushing tide over the side and see the darkening sea is choppy because streams of boats with sails and motors are cutting lines in the water, splitting the waves. They are all going the other way, out of the harbour. I hear people on the ferry boat around us asking each other exactly what I'm thinking – what is happening, where is everyone going?

I hear a voice say, "It's that humpback whale they've been talking about on the news."

I push through and find the man who said it.

"Where is it?" I say. "Where's the whale?"

"It's coming this way," he says. "It's been just outside the harbour all afternoon."

32.

"Please!" I beg Dad. "I know how to row, Grandad taught me."

Dad's home early, but he won't let me take Grandad's boat to see the whale.

"You can come with me. Or I'll take Linus. Someone can come with me, it'll be safe."

"It's not that," Dad says. "I trust you. I know you'd be fine."

There's a car reversing into our driveway, but I don't know why the man is getting out and coming over to us.

Dad asks Jodie to take me inside.

"What are you doing?" I shout.

Jodie holds my arms.

"Don't," she says. "Don't make it more difficult than it is."

I twist round. "Don't what? What's he doing?"

"Just let it go," Jodie says. "We need the money for Grandad."

I struggle out of Jodie's hands, but there's nothing I can do. Dad helps hitch the boat trailer to the man's car before it disappears down the road. It's not just Alzheimer's that's stealing all of Grandad from us. My family are *letting* people take things too.

33.

"CAN WE GO TO SEE GRANDAD NOW?" I SAY. I can't give up. "We can take him out and see the whale from the cliff across the road from there."

Dad won't say no, not now.

East Harbour Care Home smells of apple pie and yesterday. The carers don't want Grandad going across the road, no matter how much I plead. But they will let him go in the garden outside and sit in a wheelchair as the evening is warm, but he has to wear a coat and a hat and have a blanket over his knees.

I tell Grandad, over and over, that it's me, Hannah, named after the love of his life. I ask him, over and over, what did he want to tell me about the whale? What does it have to do with the deer? I point, time and time again, at the sea and tell Grandad to watch because the whale is coming. Could it be the same one that Grandad had seen before? Adam told me they could live for up to a hundred years. Did the whale remember that he'd been here before?

I'm so cross with myself that there's no power in the video camera. And even though I have the binoculars, the sea looks wide and endless from here. I see people waiting, lining the cliff top, lights on the bobbing boats below in the sea. Lifeboats and the coastguard are keeping everyone close to the harbour and near to the shore.

The sun sinks behind a streak of cloud and turns the sky and the water into fire. There's a wide golden path from here to the horizon. I wonder if Miss Bennett is looking. I wonder what she's remembering.

"Keep looking, Grandad," I say. "The whale is coming."

And it does.

I can hardly speak; my breath is caught at the top of my lungs. The whale's head rises out of the water, as if it's looking at everyone. But it's a long way out to sea, a small dark shape in the golden water. It ducks under the surface and comes up again a minute later, closer to shore. And then it dives. And we wait.

"Did you see it, Grandad? Did you see it before?"
I watch the ocean of fire in his eyes.

Even from up here we can hear voices bouncing off the sea, the murmur of everyone wanting to see it again.

We wait for another hour, but the whale has gone.

34.

Mum, Dad and Jodie take Grandad back to his room. It's getting darker and the gold of the sun has all gone, but I don't want to go inside. I hear a seagull. It sounds harsh, as if it's laughing at me. I've hardly seen any birds in our garden at home recently. Smokey has won; Smokey is full up. But I'm empty and angry.

"Did you see the whale?" a voice says. It's Mark.

He sits on the bench next to me, crosses his legs and folds his arms.

I nod.

"Oh," he says. "Don't you think it was amazing?"

"I do," I say. "But I was hoping Grandad would see it and remember me."

"The thing is," Mark says, shuffling closer, "the thing about having Alzheimer's is that your grandad doesn't really have a choice when he remembers things." I look at Mark. He has a kind face. "Then suddenly he'll remember something from long ago, even down to the tiniest details. We can give our old folks all sorts of reminders, but that doesn't guarantee anything. Sometimes a song or a photo or something on the television helps; sometimes it doesn't. But we keep trying and we're grateful when they do. But often it seems to have nothing to do with what we want."

"I thought the filming would help," I say, but it's an effort to speak. "My camera ran out of power." My eyes are still on the ocean. The boats have all gone. There is nothing there. I feel like Grandad.

"Don't give up," Mark says. "Sometimes when we're helping him dress or giving him breakfast your grandad is bright and clear and tells us snippets of his life."

I'm not sure I want to know what he says to anyone else. I can hardly make myself say it. "Like what?" I ask.

"Let me think. Oh yes, just the other day he was talking about birds... yes, birds, I'm sure it was."

"Robins?" I ask, but I daren't hope.

"Yes, robins," he smiles. "He's particularly fond of robins. He said he grows sunflowers for the birds. In fact, Jenny who comes here a few times

239

a week to do workshops has got your grandad involved in woodworking. He seems very at home using his hands."

"He used to build boats," I say. "He'd like that."

"I think they're making a bird table," he says. "Your grandad said something about keeping the birds safe from cats, but we don't have any cats around here."

I smile. I've got cold sitting outside, but suddenly I feel the warmth inside. A bird table is what we need at home. It's only something small, but it's important.

"Good to see you smile," Mark says. "Anything you think we can do to help, you just ask."

He touches my shoulder and goes to leave.

"Mark?" I say. "Grandad likes his toast cooked under the grill so it's dark with burnt bits around the edge."

"Sure," he says.

"And he likes to turn the earth for the robins, let them get at the worms. Can he have a garden fork?"

Mark laughs. "I'll see what I can do."

"And Mark? I do want to know when he remembers and I don't mind if it's you that tells me what he says instead."

All I hope now is that Grandad finds an island in his memory, somewhere familiar where he can go ashore. A place, now and again, to stop and look back across the ocean of nothing and see what he left behind. Because I'm still here, yelling for Grandad to come and get me.

35.

THE DAYS PASS. I WATCH THE NEWS, BUT THERE'S nothing more to report. The whale has gone. That's it, it's over. It feels over. Grandad is not coming home; someone else gets to share breakfast and afternoons with him. I'm upset, but I see now that no matter what I do, the Alzheimer's is bigger and stronger than me.

I go to Furze Island every day with Jodie, but

Miss Bennett's back gate has been locked and she's gone too. Adam is in the other group now so I spend the days following Jodie like a shadow. She tells me to forget about Miss Bennett.

"You've been so busy swooning around Adam that you forgot about Grandad most of the time."

"No, I haven't."

"Yes, you have. You only think about yourself and Adam."

"At least I could talk to him. At least he was nice to me."

"Grandad was always nice to you."

"But he's not now!" I can't believe how hard that hurts, but she's not finished. "Face facts, Hannah, he's not going to get better."

I'm sick of Jodie and the island. I'm starting to hate it here; it feels like I'm trapped. The video camera is charged, but there's nothing new to see.

I've run out of time anyway.

I go to the top of the steps and along the cliff top to find the hidden path down to Miss Bennett's boathouse. The door is still unlocked, from when we were in there the other day.

All I want to do is escape from here. I stare at the boat. I don't think about where I can go. I just want to leave all the emptiness and frustration behind. Furze Island is like a prison. Miss Bennett was a prisoner here, but she's escaped. *I* feel like a prisoner.

It's not that hard to push the boat on the trailer down the slope to the sea. It rolls smoothly into the waves until it floats free of the trailer. I climb in. The oars are still in their sockets. It's so easy because Grandad taught me.

I row away from the island, out into the harbour. It's mild and calm and the pushing back and forward makes me feel better. All I have to do is concentrate. I row and row, pulling, rolling and lifting. The island becomes smaller and smaller. I want it so small I can screw it up like a piece of paper and throw it in the bin. I want it so far away that it's just a speck on the horizon and I don't have to be reminded of Alzheimer's and Miss Bennett and cats any more.

I row and row and row. The sea is gentle and lets me pass through it. And then I suddenly notice how quiet it is.

I stop rowing. I'm past where the chain ferry crosses. I'm out of the harbour, at sea.

It's peaceful, like I've rowed all my frustration away, like the sea has given me its calmness, and everything that was bothering me is out of my sight. But I see the water all around me and I feel smaller than ever. I'm alone. And then what I think of is Grandad, as if he might be in a boat somewhere out here.

But there are no other boats. I could stand and yell for Grandad, but he's not going to come and get me, is he?

My heart swells and my eyes fill. I weep on my arms. I don't want to think about the past. I don't want to know about the future.

And then I hear a soft puff. There is a smell, like mackerel fish. I hear a gulp in the water beside me. Then quiet. The soft puff comes again and gentle rain falls over me. The fishy smell is strong now.

I turn to the side. I see an eye, gentle and wrinkled. I see deep grooves and the circles of white barnacles as the whale comes alongside the boat. His huge body is lying just under the water. I jump back and fall off the seat, knocking one of the oars into the sea. I am breathing hard, lying on the bottom of the boat, hiding, and then all I think is, what am I doing? I crawl over and pick up the video camera and switch it on. I take a deep breath and kneel up and peer through the lens over the side. I can't move; my eyes are wide open and my heart is bursting. The whale is looking at me.

I see his spout close and feel a gentle lap as a wave rocks the boat. He puffs again. The whale seems to be waiting.

I don't even know if the whale has ears, but I keep the camera switched on and talk to him anyway.

I laugh because somehow I'm not scared to talk to this giant. "I know he's not in the sea," I say, "but I'm looking for my grandad here anyway. But instead I found you."

I laugh again because the whale stays. "Do you know my grandad?"

The whale ducks, but comes up again, making a soft fountain over me. He is looking right at me.

I reach my hand and the whale stays steady beside me. I touch his skin. It's like rubber.

"Grandad's not as big as you." I think about that. It's not always the size of something that makes it have a big effect. "But he's still the biggest thing I know."

The whale waits for a moment and it's the longest moment I've ever known. Looking into that whale's eye.

"My grandad's name is Arthur Jenkins. Did you ever see him? Did he ever see you?"

The whale blinks.

I swivel round and point the camera at the mainland coast, to the east.

"He's up there." I point to the cliff top on the mainland. "We watched you." Then I remember that Grandad didn't seem to see, not really. "But you were too far away." I turn the camera back to the whale. "I've got you on film now, close up, and I'll show him and maybe sometime he'll remember what he wanted to tell me."

The whale dips gently under the water, so he doesn't make waves or suck the boat under. His vast shadow disappears into the deep green. I scrabble about the boat, looking over the sides, but I can't see him any more. Then just ahead of me I see the surface break, just where my oar has floated away. The whale has the oar and nudges it, closer and closer, until I can reach out... and then everything seems to stop. My heart is wide open as I reach for the oar, just as Grandad had reached out that time in the care home, just like the statue on the quay.

I see the whale's knowing eye before he silently dips below the sea.

36.

I ROW BACK TO THE ISLAND AND PUT THE BOAT away. My arms and back are tired, but inside I'm buzzing with energy, with what I've got to show Grandad.

I hadn't noticed before, but there's an envelope just inside the door of the boathouse with my name on it. I guess it's from Miss Bennett, saying goodbye. There are also two photographs. One is of me in Miss Bennett's boat. The other is of two children in a boat, on a misty morning. A girl has her arms wrapped round a young deer on her lap, a boy is rowing. I can't see their faces; the girl's is turned down and the boy has his back to us, his wide shoulders pulling on the oars.

My mouth is open and it feels like a jigsaw is collecting, assembling and making a picture before my eyes. I recognise Grandad's boat. Is that my grandad and grandma in it?

Both of the photos are signed Eva Bennett. The one of me is dated a few days ago. The other August 18th 1942.

I look for Jodie. I hold the camera in the air. "I found the whale!" I laugh and wave the photographs.

I tell her I have to show Grandad, that I'm catching the ferry back and going to East Harbour

Care Home on the bus. I thought she'd be glad to be alone with Adam again. His name doesn't make her go all dopey. Her lips aren't glossy, her eyes are not sparkling.

"Don't you like Adam any more?"

"He's more interested in himself, I think." She shrugs and sighs, but she doesn't seem upset. "He gave all the girls a *special* piece of driftwood."

That's why she's been so moody. She loved Adam, but he didn't love her. "It wasn't love then, not really."

Jodie laughs. "You sound like Grandad. Just go," she says. "I'll cover for you."

On the bus I read what I think is Miss Bennett's goodbye letter.

Dearest Hannah,

I know you wanted to find out more about Fern, and so after our marvellous trip in my boat I found the photograph which you should now have.

The night decoy bombs on Furze Island were exploded, I wasn't the only one who stayed out of the air-raid shelter on the mainland.

I saw the deer take to the water to escape the fire. Confused by the smoke, they swam out of the harbour. My boat was still on the island and there was nothing I could do. I watched and waited all night for the smoke to clear.

Just before dawn, when the bombing had stopped, I saw a small boat coming from over the quiet side of the harbour, heading towards Hambourne slipway. This is the photograph I took of the children in that boat who had rowed out to sea and brought Fern back with them.

They asked me if I would take care of her, made me promise not to tell anyone what they had done. They knew they were in trouble for staying out of the air-raid shelter, and didn't want their parents to worry. And I kept my promise. I named the deer Fern after my grandmother, whom I'd loved very much.

Fern stayed with me on the mainland until the war was over and I could move back into my family home on the island. She was all I had left.

I thought those children might have come back with terrible memories like me from that awful night, fearful of the things that they had seen and would never forget. But that wasn't the case. They were rather secretive and would only say that it wasn't them that saved the deer.

Yours,

Eva Bennett

I collect all the little pieces together in my mind, all the memories from different people and my own. I don't think for a minute that I've got it wrong this time. I know Grandad. My grandma and grandad stayed out of the air-raid shelter, filling their ears with the sound of the bombers, filling their hearts by trying to rescue the deer. They must have followed the deer out to sea and brought Fern back with them. I know it's exactly what he would have done.

I imagine Grandad and Grandma going back to the island every year, to remember that night again and again. August 18th.

And since Grandma died, Grandad had been back to see the deer for himself, to remember her.

A strong memory scoops me up. Sitting on Grandad's lap after eating too much chocolate, asking him if he married Grandma when she was a little girl. *Something great put us together… and it will never be undone.*

I watch my film of the whale on the small screen. And I wonder what really bound two children together in the middle of a war, in the dark, far out at sea all by themselves.

I feel Grandad is with me. He's in *my* memory, *my* heart, in all the places so small we can't see them, but so big they are what make us who we are. I laugh out loud and the lady in front of me on the bus turns round to look at me.

"My grandad took me on a journey and I found a whale," I say.

"Where have you been?" she says.

"Not far," I smile. "Some journeys are really close to home."

I see the whale on the tiny screen. I see him rise, the oar being lifted out of the water. I think of the mistakes I've made when I didn't look, didn't see properly, like thinking a sandbar was a whale. Is it too big and extraordinary to think what I'm thinking? Could Fern have thought the whale was an island too?

37.

GRANDAD ISN'T IN HIS ROOM.

"He's outside in the garden," Mark says, leaning against the doorpost. "He hasn't wanted to come inside all day, as if he's waiting for someone. Go and see what he's made for you."

There's a smell of newly cut wood. A tall bird table is outside, just what we need to keep the birds safe from Smokey.

Grandad is in a wheelchair; he's looking out to sea, but strangely I have nothing to say. I was going to show Grandad the film, but now I'm here I don't need to. It's as if seeing the whale has changed something in me. The whale was so peaceful, so gentle and so huge, and I can't think of anything bigger than what I feel now. And besides, when I follow Grandad's eyes and see what he's looking at, I know there's only one thing left to do.

I look back at Mark. "Go on, go," he says. "I won't say a word."

I push Grandad in the wheelchair across the road and down a path from the cliff top to a ledge just above the coastline. I put the brake on the wheelchair and think about turning the video camera on, but I don't. I want to make another vivid memory of my own.

I stand beside Grandad and hold his hand. He squeezes mine back.

"Grandad, it's August the eighteenth."

"Yes… I remember," he says.

"And I'll always remember for you too. And for Grandma."

I crouch beside him. I can hardly say what I want to say out loud, it's far too extraordinary. "Grandad? Who saved the deer?"

Grandad's ancient smile gathers in his cheeks and I see what made him who he is. "The whale," he whispers.

The thing about a journey is not that you find something so exciting, so marvellous that you can't wait to tell everyone. The end of the journey is when none of it matters. All I know is I love my grandad. As he is now. I've been on my own journey to find the greatest power on earth. And I did and I know what it is now. Love. Not something from the past, but what I have now. That's the important thing that keeps us going, no matter what happens. It's what makes us think bigger.

My heart feels as big as a whale's. So big that everything else seems small and insignificant.

The whale is here, close to shore. We are waving; we want him to see us up here. I think he looks up towards us. He turns and dives; his wishbone tail hovers for a moment before it gently falls into the sea.

"Do you think he came back to see you, Grandad?" I say.

"I think he came to see you." Grandad says. I laugh and he laughs, because just for a minute he's right here with me. And that's enough.

"Look how you've grown," Grandad says.

I think of our sunflowers. I feel giant like them.

As if Grandad has called the whale back again, he rises out of the sea in front of us. I know the gentle wrinkles around his eye. He ducks under. We wait.

The whale breaks the surface again and the sea crashes open wide. And I can't help catching my breath when the long curve of his great grey back erupts like a mountain out of the sea. He leaps high and it's suddenly silent and peaceful. For me too. I feel his cool shadow sheltering me. The air smells of sea salt. I can taste the brine. The whale reaches to the sky and my mouth is open wide in wonder at the giant in front of us. And then the sea bursts as he smashes deep into the water.

He's just like my grandad.

Acknowledgments

I think stories come from stories, and there are people who have contributed their personal experiences to this one, whether directly or indirectly. I'm indebted to my octogenarian friend and neighbour Brenda Carr, Richard Bonham Christie, Sam Swinnerton, and it was my good fortune to know another octogenarian, Ted Alsop, whose stories will be missed. Thank you to the 'village' of people at HarperCollins for making another dream come true, especially my editor, Rachel Denwood, who understands the better story. Everlasting thanks for the continued support of family, friends and my agent, Julia Churchill.

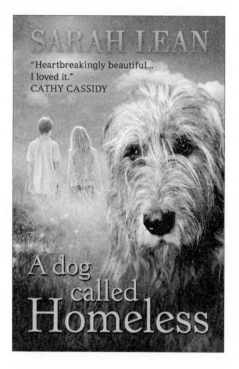

SARAH LEAN

"Heartbreakingly beautiful...
I loved it."
CATHY CASSIDY

A dog
called
Homeless

My name is Cally Louise Fisher
and I haven't spoken for thirty-one days.
Talking doesn't always make things happen,
however much you want it to.

Cally saw her mum, bright and real and alive.
But no one believes her, so Cally stopped talking.
Now a mysterious grey wolfhound has started
following her everywhere. Perhaps he knows that
Cally was telling the truth...

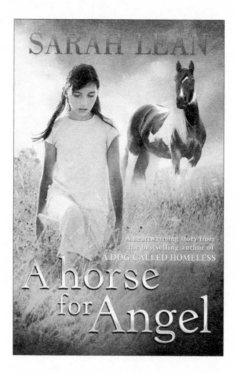

Sometimes when things are broken
you can't fix them on your own –
no matter how hard you try.

When Nell is sent to stay with distant family,
she packs a suitcase full of secrets. A chance
encounter with a wild horse draws Nell to Angel
– a mysterious, troubled girl who is hiding secrets
of her own. Both girls must learn to trust each
other, if they are to save a hundred horses…